Mistakenly in Mallorca

Roderic Jeffries

Table of Contents

CHAPTER I   5
CHAPTER II   12
CHAPTER III   18
CHAPTER IV   25
CHAPTER V   29
CHAPTER VI   39
CHAPTER VII   51
CHAPTER VIII   60
CHAPTER IX   67
CHAPTER X   72
CHAPTER XI   79
CHAPTER XII   89
CHAPTER XIII   92
CHAPTER XIV   100
CHAPTER XV   108
CHAPTER XVI   115
CHAPTER XVII   121
CHAPTER XVIII   129
CHAPTER XIX   137
CHAPTER XX   147
CHAPTER XXI   152
CHAPTER XXII   156
CHAPTER XXIII   160
CHAPTER XXIV   168

CHAPTER XXV

CHAPTER I

EIGHT DAYS LATER, John Tatham was to remember the words with bitterness, but at the time they were acceptable. 'There's no need to worry, sir. We'll look after her.' Of course the police would. That was what part of their job was all about. 'Thank goodness for that,' he'd said, and moved on to worry about a cow that was calving to a premium bull and was overdue.

'Lovely-looking herd you've got out in the paddock,' the policeman had said. 'My father was head cowman to Sir Alfred, so I know.'

Without any idea who Sir Alfred might be, he'd warmed to the words, but they should have made him suspicious about the value of the assurances he'd just been given. To any expert eye, his herd was uneven — small wonder since he'd not the money to buy top, or even second, quality. Some of the cows gave eight hundred gallons only by straining and were really fit for little but the dog-meat slaughterhouse.

'Well,' the policeman had said, and he'd slapped his leather gauntlets against his long, dark blue, regulation raincoat, 'I'll be on my way. And not to worry: no harm'll come to her. Mark my words.'

As a fortune-teller, the policeman rated C3. He'd given a friendly wave that was part informal salute, put on crash helmet, mounted his Noddy bike, and left.

The cow had calved around midnight, two hours after the vet arrived, and the calf was dead. Just one of those things, the vet had said. But for him it had meant a potential fifty-pound loss when every penny counted.

Still, he'd been assured that Jennifer would be all right.

*

The bank was at the lower end of the high street, sandwiched between a cheapjack furniture shop and a hairdresser. Built in Georgian style, it had been given graceful proportions which were now entirely wasted because developers had, in twelve years, turned the old high street into a concrete and plate glass architectural chamber of horrors. Outside, the wide road had recently been divided into two with the oneway traffic restricted to the outer lane and the near one kept for buses and unloading vans. Inside, the

5

bank had been modernized to the extent of providing bullet-proof glass screens along the top of the long public counter to protect the tellers.

Invest, said the posters on the walls facing the tellers: unit trusts, deposit accounts, property bonds. As Jennifer paid out and received money day after day, she knew she was not going to invest in anything but cows. In her bank deposit account were seven hundred and sixty-three pounds forty, enough to buy three and a half cows (choose the end where the milk comes from, John had told her) of top breeding which would form the nucleus of a herd that would become famed. Not that she liked cows. They were big, clumsy, stupid, and the one time she'd tried to give a hand milking she'd been splattered with tish. But John thought there was nothing in the world more lovely than a broad-backed, smoothly-bagged Friesian which bettered fifteen hundred gallons every lactation.

Friday the thirteenth — the superstitious were quick to notice that — began as just another Friday. Report for work, draw the float and sign for it, prepare the till, explain to the chief cashier what the hurriedly written note of the previous day meant, see that the latest list of stolen and stopped cheques was pinned up, that the scales were ready and the weights had not been borrowed by one of the other tellers, listen to a whispered story about a girl she knew vaguely who'd gone to a party and ... She didn't believe it. Then it was nine-thirty and the outer doors were opened to the public.

'What's it like, handling so much money?' John had once asked her when he hadn't been thinking about cows. She didn't regard it as money. It was a commodity of little variety, basically useless, which had to be balanced out at the end of a day. Only occasionally did this sense of detachment cease. The 'tramp' had indirectly shattered it. Two days' growth of beard, reddened eyes, no tie, collarless shirt, badly patched jacket, and a cheque made out to cash for three hundred and fifty pounds. She'd taken the cheque to the chief cashier who'd smiled and said that Mr MacVitie might look to be worth no more than a farthing (the chief cashier was old-fashioned in most things) but if he presented a cheque for a thousand he'd not be draining his account. She'd turned round, to go back to her counter, and she'd faced a man with a sawn-off shotgun.

The raid was well planned and had the benefit of simplicity. Four men, wearing security guard uniforms, helmets on their heads, goggles over their eyes, entered the bank. Security guards had become such a feature of life that no one took special note of them or stopped to ponder on the coincidence that each of them had a thick, bushy moustache which effectively concealed much of the remaining portion of his face not already concealed by goggles and helmet. Each carried a long, narrow case. Nos. 1 and 2 went to the information desk, No. 3 remained by the door, No. 4 passed Nos. 1 and 2 and swung open the three-foot barrier which gave access to the working part of the bank. The foreign-currency clerk stood up and asked No. 4 if he could help, in a tone of voice which demanded an explanation of why he was doing what he was doing. No. 4 opened his case and pulled out a sawn-off shotgun and the others did the same. No. 1 moved smoothly, using the same swing door as No. 4, to stand amongst the desks to cover the staff, No. 2 remained where he was, and No. 3 remained by the side of the outer door to cover the customers already in the bank and any more who entered. Two of the tellers pressed the panic buttons under the long counter.

Jennifer shrieked.

No. 4 came out of the manager's office, forcing the manager ahead of him, and there was a trickle of blood coursing down the right-hand side of the manager's head. No. 2 joined him and they went down the stairs to the strong-room in the basement below.

Rigby, a member of the bank's regional rugby team, acted courageously but recklessly. He threw himself at No. 1 in a tackle and was immediately shot, at such close range that despite the drastically shortened barrels the whole column of shot thudded into his back. He crashed to the floor and his feet kept up a constant drumming until he died. No. 1 reloaded the right-hand barrel immediately, pushing home a fresh cartridge even as the ejected empty one, smoking, arced over his shoulder. In a gesture of nervousness he twisted his head sideways and briefly a small scar, star-shaped, was visible on his neck.

Nos. 4 and 2 ran up from the strong-room, carrying three khaki canvas sacks in each hand, their guns strung through homemade holsters at their sides. They left the banking area by the swing barrier and No. 1 followed them. No. 3 joined them as they went outside. The gathering crowd parted with a violent surge that left two women on the pavement. The bank robbers ran to the security van parked immediately in front of the bank, two climbed into the cab, two into the rear compartment, and they drove off, crashed the lights, and disappeared. The first police car arrived ninety seconds later.

'Oh God!' muttered Jennifer, as she stared down at Rigby. She didn't then know he was dying, but the drumming feet and the bloody, mangled area of his back made her sick.

*

'I know how you must feel,' said the detective-constable with sympathetic firmness, 'but I've got to question you whilst it's all fresh in your mind.'

She gripped Tatham's hand more tightly, demanding and getting comfort. 'I ... I'm sorry to be like this, but it's so ... I'd been speaking to Ernest only a few minutes before.'

'I'm afraid this sort of thing always is a terrible shock. I can remember ...' He told the tale well. It somehow usually calmed down a witness to be reminded that his or her tragedy was not unique.

Tatham looked at his watch, not as surreptitiously as he'd hoped.

'I'll be all right now, darling,' she said, understanding that the needs of his animals had to be more important than her fears.

'It's OK for another half-hour.'

She longed to tell him what a wonderful help he was being, but the presence of the detective inhibited her. But at least she could look at his rough-hewn face — 'You'll never make the central spread of *Cosmopolitan*' — and love it for its obvious strength and kindness.

'Now, miss,' said the detective, 'just tell me precisely what you did from the time you arrived. Never mind how small the details or that they're what happen every day. I want to build up the complete picture and that includes all normal routine.'

She described her arrival, the few minutes in the ladies' cloakroom, the story about the girl she'd known, the first customer, the 'tramp' and why she'd left her seat and gone to speak to the chief cashier who worked in one of the open-style cubicles, the man with the gun. She'd been frightened cold. Ernest had suddenly thrown himself forward in a rugby-style tackle and had been shot. He'd thudded to the ground, his back a bloody mess, his feet drumming. The gunman had reloaded. He'd twisted his head round in what had looked like a nervous gesture and that odd-shaped scar ...

'Odd-shaped scar?' said the detective sharply.

She was rather bewildered. Until that moment she hadn't realized she'd seen a scar.

*

'A star-shaped scar, perhaps an inch across, on the right-hand side of the neck about two inches below the jaw,' repeated the sergeant in Records. 'Man about five foot ten or eleven, well built, no other physical features observable. Carrying sawn-off shotgun for a bank raid and shooting without hesitation. OK, I've got all that. I'll do what I can, sir, but it'll take a bit of time … I know, sir, but with a rather meagre description …' The sergeant finally replaced the telephone. 'If he can do it so much better, why the hell doesn't he come here and show us how?'

*

The magistrates' court, built in 1931, wras pretentious in style and poor in acoustics. The magistrates sat on the dais in high-backed, gilded, velvet-covered chairs.

The chairman was a solid, formless woman, with a face like old parchment, a voice of baffling superiority, and a double row of genuine pearls around her wattled neck. 'You say you do not want to give the address of this witness in open court, but wish to write it down and hand it to the bench?'

'Yes, your worship,' said prosecuting solicitor.

'For what reason?'

'The police have reason to believe that friends of the accused may try to intimidate the witness, your worship, should they learn her address.'

The chairman, together with her three fellow magistrates, looked at Jennifer. They saw a slim, pleasantly attractive but unremarkable woman in her middle twenties, dressed neatly in clothes of no particular elegance, who was nervously fiddling with the thin belt of her dress.

The chairman was a woman of strong character, but in one respect rather stupid (stupidity had never been a bar to becoming a magistrate in an English court): she believed it far more important rigidly to observe procedure than to worry about the human side of justice. 'Have any threats actually been made?'

'Not yet, your worship, and it is to avoid the possibility …'

'The whole matter, then, is supposition and not fact?'

Surely even she could realize the two men in the dock — their two companions on the bank raid were still unidentified — were right villains, eager to take any steps to escape conviction? thought the prosecuting solicitor. When the evidence was closely studied by the defence lawyers, it would be only too clear how important a part of the prosecution's case was this witness's evidence.

9

'Justice should be carried out under the harsh light of full disclosure of facts,' said the chairman. She turned and briefly murmured to her fellow magistrates on either side of her, then addressed the prosecuting solicitor again: 'The witness will give her address in open court. The police are quite capable of dealing with anyone malicious or stupid enough to try in any way to intimidate the witness.'

'But your worship ...'

'We will not hear any further argument on that score.'

*

'There's no need to worry,' said the uniformed constable, wearing long blue regulation mackintosh because although the early October day was fine, the wind was cold, especially when riding a motor-bike.

Tatham had been worrying a great deal, but this policeman, bluff, cheerful, had assured him that he was worrying unecessarily. 'Thank goodness for that.' One worry was replaced by another. The cow was getting weaker and looked as if she might go down. If the calf didn't start soon, he'd have to call in the vet.

*

Jennifer could not have known she was going to die until the last second.

On Friday, some shops stayed open late and she usually did the weekend shopping for herself and her widowed mother after tea. She parked her Mini not far from Sains-bury's new supermarket and walked to the high street and then up to a draper's to get some needles and wool for her mother. On her way back to the supermarket, she bought a woman's magazine because it had a long article on preparing to be a bride. Not that she wasn't prepared. John was the one who hesitated, because he still couldn't be certain he'd make the farm yield up a living and she couldn't persuade him that she didn't give a twopenny damn about an obvious lack of security.

When she left the supermarket, with a small piece of meat, some beans, a bottle of chutney, two apple yoghurts, a packet of Cheddar cheese, a treacle tart, and a jar of instant coffee, she turned left by the lights and started down the four hundred yards to the car park.

At the music shop she stopped briefly to stare at the hi-fi set in the centre display. If she won the pools or the premium bonds, she'd buy that set and dozens and dozens of records. If. She walked on until opposite the car park, then started to cross the road.

There was a roar of unleashed power and a car, previously parked on the solid yellow lines, accelerated away from the pavement with smoking tyres. She turned and saw it coming straight at her and hesitated, shocked by such appalling driving. Then, at the last second, she realized the truth.

The car hit her, jerked her feet from under her so that her head smashed back into the bonnet, flung her sideways into a concrete light standard. She was dead by the time she was admitted to hospital.

CHAPTER II

JOHN TATHAM had inherited the ability to dream great dreams from his father and the staying power to try to turn those dreams into reality from his mother. No one could even guess from whom he'd inherited his love of farming since he came from generations of city dwellers.

'Only millionaires and fools go into farming today,' had said his uncle. Uncle Harold was on the commodity market, very successful, very wealthy, and like all successful, wealthy men certain of his own infallibility. He was also ashamed of having as a brother a not very successful painter who seldom wore a tie, owned only one suit, and laughed at many of the things which really mattered in life: safe capital, the right friends, clever accountants, tailored pension schemes.

'So you'd better join my firm,' Uncle Harold had continued, 'and earn a respectable living.' When his offer had been refused, with thanks, he had been bitter because the rich do not like to be denied the chance of gaining merit in the eyes of the world.

John Tatham spent three years in an agricultural college where he learned, amongst other things, that Uncle Harold had been partially right because without a great deal of capital it was now virtually impossible to farm on one's own account. Land cost a thousand pounds an acre, yet the return from farming was so low that it wasn't worth more than a couple of hundred pounds an acre to someone trying to make a living from it. In any case, borrowing large sums of money had become ridiculously expensive. There were still farms to let, though they were becoming fewer and fewer, but the large ones called for a great deal of equipment and years of practical experience and the small ones were, generally speaking, either too small to be economic or else of very poor quality.

His inherited determination and staying power supported him while he worked on as a farm labourer and in his spare time searched the country for a small farm to rent. Eventually, he found Sadacre Farm, owned by a local council, up for renting by tender. The farm was all a farm shouldn't be: too small, useless buildings, unsuited to modern dairy farming, heavy clay undrained and lacking any humus or fertility and fit only for growing

Yorkshire Fog. But his father's powers of dreaming set to work and he saw modern buildings, hedges cut, land drained, tons of muck per acre turning the yellow clay friable, rye grass thick … He tendered a high rent and became the tenant.

Sadacre Farm had been well named, no doubt by one of the embittered men who'd once tried to farm it and failed. He worked all hours God made, adapted and modernized buildings — in so far as this was possible — built a side-by-side milking parlour, cow kennels, and a Dutch barn from telegraph poles and second-hand corrugated iron, bought cows and machinery on the HP, and milked three times a day to get the last possible extra pound of milk.

In the rain, the land lay waterlogged; in the dry, it set like concrete. Hedges had been so neglected that when cut back they let stock through. Calves died, for no discernible reason. Mastitis was rife, no matter how careful he was milking out and washing the bags. There was an endemic cough which wasn't husk and which the vet couldn't identify, but which cut milk badly. Machinery broke down, always at the most inconvenient moment — two acres of hay to bale and black-bellied clouds rolling up.

In his third year at Sadacre Farm, he went to a dance — his first night out in months — and there he met Jennifer. She didn't like cows, but she liked to hear him talk about them. And she liked to look at his rugged, chunky face, expressing practical determination with a dreamy background, to stroke his cheeks, to have him engulf her in his arms and feel the strength of his body. She also liked it when he became passionate and after a while she'd be for forgetting everything but the immediate present: but he was strangely old-fashioned in this respect and thought they ought to wait until they were married. 'All right,' she'd said one evening, filled with unladylike frustration, 'but only if you'll marry me soon so maybe you'll learn there's more to sex than the row a bulling cow makes.'

He wanted to get married just as much as she did, but he didn't feel justified in marrying her until he could offer her a more secure future.

By now, he knew for fact what he'd always believed — he was a good dairy farmer. He had a way with animals, a feel for the land, and mechanical sympathy. All that held him back was lack of capital. He naively thought that, since he had learned his trade, Uncle Harold might help him.

Uncle Harold was delighted to be asked. He loved delivering sermons. Hadn't he always said farming was a ridiculous occupation? How many farmers ever became wealthy from farming alone? Now coffee, sugar, cocoa, copper, tin, lead, zinc — provided some underpaid worker grew or mined them and you were the middleman who milked the market (Rather subtle, what?) — made real money. But his advice had been rejected years before and it had always been his strongly held belief that if a man insisted on making his own bed, he should be left to lie on it ...

'Bloody pompous old fool,' said Jennifer. 'Hope his cocoa poisons him and his sugar turns sour.' She put her arms round his neck and stared straight at his strong blue eyes. 'John, you are an infuriating person because you're more stubborn than a team of mules. I've told you millions of times, I don't care if life's tough: I just want to be with you, whether we sleep in silk sheets or old sacks. So now I'm going to be stubborn. I'm going to marry you, whether you like it or not, in six months' time, because I can't wait a day longer. But I do ask that you don't milk the cows that morning because my wedding day is going to be one day when there's no cow tish around.'

He grinned. 'So I've got my orders?'

'You've got 'em and I expect total obedience. And now kiss me hard, but not for too long or I'll not be able to wait those six months.'

Five weeks later, she was dead.

*

He was filling the feed barrow with crushed barley and concentrate, just before milking for the last time that day, when a policeman in blue mackintosh, crash helmet, and leather boots, entered the building and stood by the side of the chart on which were listed the dates of cows' bullings and services. He noticed the expression on the policeman's face and he became scared.

He dropped the scoop into the mixture and walked very deliberately over to where the policeman stood, identifying him as the man who had called before. 'Evening. Is something wrong?'

'I ... I've some bad news for you, sir.'

'What?' he demanded flatly.

The policeman spoke quickly. 'Miss Payne has unfortunately been in an accident: she was knocked down by a car just off the High Street.'

Tatham said, quite levelly: 'Is she dead?'

The policeman nodded.

'Was it an accident? Or did the men behind the bank robbery kill her?'

'The car didn't stop and it ... it sounds deliberate.'

'So you were wrong. There was need to worry about her. The police couldn't look after her.'

The policeman, suffering the other's bitter contempt, knew a sudden resentment. It hadn't been his fault.

'Where is she?'

'She was taken to the general hospital.'

There was a thud against the sliding door of the collecting yard as the lead cow tried to force the door open. 'I must start milking,' Tatham said.

The policeman left, wondering how any man could be so insensitive as to be able to milk cows only minutes after he'd been told his fiancée was dead. He didn't realize that cows had to be milked no matter what human tragedies exploded, nor had he any idea that Tatham was crying as he let the first cows into the parlour.

*

Felicity Tatham was a delightful woman of 55 who enjoyed having a husband who'd refused to make a lot of money in the City, but who instead painted pictures and made very little. He was happy so she was happy, so that was what life was about. Let the Harolds of the world make fortunes, losing in the process all the fun of living.

She looked across the very small sitting-room of the farmhouse in which she and her husband lived. 'You should have come back here much sooner, John,' she said softly. It hurt to see the lines of strain in his face.

'I thought about it and decided not to,' he answered. 'I needed to be on my own until I knew my mind.'

He'd always acted the same way, she thought. When hurt as a boy, either physically or mentally, he'd withdrawn and hugged his hurt to himself. In his case it denoted a strength of character, but she was sorry he was like that because the hurt dug so much deeper. 'Has it been very bad?' she asked, trying to make him talk about it and so release some of the pressures inside his mind.

'Bad enough.' He stared into space. 'The funny thing is, I still sometimes find myself believing she'll drive up in that broken-down Mini of hers. Then I have to remind myself that I went to her funeral.' He took a pack of cigarettes from his pocket and offered it to her, so deep in his own sad thoughts he forgot she never smoked. He lit the cigarette. 'When it was all over, one of the things I had to do was work out my future plans.' He focused his gaze on her. 'You know, a thing like this makes one look at life in pretty harsh colours and I suddenly saw Sadacre Farm for what it really was: a place that couldn't ever respond to modern intensive farming because it just wasn't up to it.'

He rolled the cigarette round in his fingers. 'Of course, I'd never imagined it could be a show place, but at the same time I'd gone on kidding myself I could eventually make of it something reasonable that would see us through the first few years until we got something better: rose-tinted spectacles, if you like. Her death made me throw those spectacles away and see the place just exactly as it was. A hopeless proposition.'

'Don't you think you may be painting everything a little too grey?' she asked tentatively. 'After a terrible tragedy ...'

'No.'

She remembered the pride with which, two years before, he'd told her about his breeding policy, the yields promised by the latest strains of grass especially bred for heavy land, and his other ideas which were all filled with the flush of enthusiastic ambition. Yet now he sounded like someone who'd reached the end of his working career.

'I've packed the farm in,' he said suddenly. 'Given up the lease.'

'Oh no!' she said automatically, but with deep feeling.

'It wasn't only seeing the farm without my spectacles on. It was having to fight all the memories. The chip in the wall where she'd lost control of the feed barrow when she was trying to help me so we could get to the flicks in time for the last performance, the square of land where she planned a greenhouse, the cow with the crumpled horn which she kept saying ought to go up to the moon in the next spacecraft ...'

'Do you mean you're giving up all your stock as well?'

'I've got rid of everything.'

She sighed.

'You think I've been stupid?' he asked. 'But I couldn't stay on there, not with all those memories, not when I no longer believed in my own ambitions.'

'Of course not,' she agreed, silently wondering whether he was right. If only she'd been with him to help, perhaps things would not have looked so black? He might not have reacted so drastically? 'So what are you going to do now?'

He shrugged his shoulders. 'Start again somewhere else — if I can find anywhere else. Or get a job as a tractor-driver or cowman and hope to make farm manager one day.'

'But not before you've had a break from everything and everybody here.'

'How d'you mean?'

'Get out of this country, John. There's Aunt Elvina who lives somewhere in Mallorca. Go and stay with her. She's a queer old stick, but it would be a complete change and that's what you need.'

He shrugged his shoulders.

Typically, she was determined to get things moving as soon as possible. 'Your father can phone her tonight. She always seemed to have a soft spot for him so I'm sure she'll agree.'

He looked at his watch and just for a second he thought he must get a move on if he was to milk the cows on time.

CHAPTER III

'HAROLD,' said Elvina Woods in a pugnacious tone of voice, 'is a fool. So's that ninny of a wife of his.'

The portable gas heater had all three panels alight, yet even so Tatham was only just warm enough, largely because the sitting-room was fifteen feet high. A meeting between Elvina and Harold would be worth watching, he thought. Harold was pedantic and as cheerful as a picnic in the pouring rain. Elvina had all the charm of total unpredictability, was rough of tongue, ate and drank with gusto, and was tremendous fun provided one was not easily embarrassed.

'He heard I was coming out here to live and then had the neck to give me his unasked-for advice. Don't come because there'll be another civil war. He's the kind of man who sees civil wars under his bed … You can get me another brandy, John, with a little less soda this time.'

It would be difficult to add much less soda, he thought, as he stood up and took the glass from her. He went through to the kitchen and turned right into the larder. Both kitchen and larder were recent additions, built on to the back of the three-hundred-year-old finca. Typically, no damp course had been installed so that rising damp had blotched the walls with a grey-black fungus up to a height of a metre. According to the published statistics, Elvina had told him, it practically never rained on the island — unfortunately, the weather couldn't read. He poured out a large brandy and added the merest splash of soda.

'Tomorrow,' said Elvina, on his return to the sitting-room, 'we're invited to the Eastmores' reception. I said we'd go because I know she doesn't want me to.'

'That sounds a very good reason.'

'When you've met her, you'll realize it is.'

'She's the woman you often talk about?'

'The infuriating thing is, one does often talk about her. She's got what in my day was called a presence. She undoubtedly kept the natives in their place when she was the governor's wife, but I can't think why one of them didn't cut her throat. God knows how Charles, her husband, puts up with her: after all, he's human.'

'But she isn't?'

'Emotionally, certainly not. She reminds me of a relative of mine who had an acute attack of appendicitis in church, but wouldn't do a thing about it until the sermon was over, out of respect to God. I told her, if that's how God wanted you to behave, He's got some queer ideas.'

'And how did she accept that?'

'She called me a wicked woman and in her will took a whole paragraph explaining why she wasn't leaving me a penny.'

'The moral being, you should have praised her fortitude, not called her an ass!'

'And no doubt Mary Eastmore believes she should be praised for doing her chilly duty when she tries to dictate all our lives by precept. But you know as well as I do, John, most of the trouble in this world is caused by people with a holier-than-thou attitude ... Why the hell should I have my hair permed as if I was twenty? If I want it looking like a hayfield, that's how I want it.'

'Then it's become as much an affectation as some you're complaining about.'

She stared at him for several seconds, then laughed loudly. 'By God, you're a different chap from your Uncle Harold and his tribe. Bloody nincompoops, the lot of 'em.'

He wondered how the other English on the island referred to her. Judging by some of the people he'd met, only in tones of outraged incomprehension. She was an eccentric. She had a square face which looked much squarer than it need have done because she never bothered to go to a hairdresser but had Catalina, the maid, cut her hair when it grew long enough to bother her: her body was lumpy, but she wore little or no corseting and her clothes might all have been bought at a church jumble sale: her shoes were usually in a state of disrepair. The conventional response to such an appearance must be to name it slatternly. Yet he knew that she was no slattern. Her appearance reflected her casual disregard for unimportant matters (or what she considered unimportant) and her contempt for those who believed appearances were all that mattered. His mother had told him that she'd always been unusual, but her determination deliberately to flout conventional standards had only come after the relatively early death of her husband.

She lit a small cigar and smoked it with enjoyment. 'Why did you suddenly go in for farming?' she suddenly asked. 'There can't be a farmer in the family for generations back.'

The question had the unfortunate result of jerking his mind back to England and memories of Jennifer. 'I've no idea why — it's just what I wanted to do,' he replied shortly.

'Are you any good at it?'

'Yes, I am.'

'So you don't suffer from false modesty?'

'Why should I?'

She regarded him shrewdly. She saw the lines of hurt around his strong mouth and knew he was remembering the past, but harsh experience had taught her that to talk about it might offer some relief. 'Tell me about your farm.'

Initially, he'd intended to give her only the barest description. But as soon as he began to speak the words came in a rush. He'd known the farm was in poor heart, but beggars couldn't be choosers and he'd thought that if he worked hard enough he'd make a go of it. He described the struggle it had been to get started, the sympathetic but all too realistic farm manager, the second-hand machinery which kept breaking down but was all he could afford, the cows which weren't of top breeding because these cost so much more, the soil which seemed to possess every known disadvantage ... And he described the final disillusionment which followed Jennifer's death.

'I can see why you farm and why you're good,' she said quietly, with a great depth of compassionate understanding. 'But what happens now when you return home?'

'I'll look for another place to rent, or get a job on one and work up to a farm manager.'

'Would that suit you?'

'Not really.'

'Then why not buy a place that would reward you properly for all your work?'

'Because of the money involved. As Uncle Harold said, only millionaires or fools farm nowadays.'

'That's just the kind of pretentious bilge he would mutter. How big a farm would you choose?'

'As a dairy farm? Between a hundred and fifty and two hundred acres. Some people say that's too small, but I reckon the future is in small units, just big enough to be economic and which can be run efficiently, rather than very large units which aren't ever run really efficiently.'

'And if you had two hundred acres, you'd make a success of things?'

'Inside five years, I'd have as good an average milk yield as anyone.'

'I like a man who can make a sober assessment of his own capabilities,' she said in mocking tones, but she smiled at him.

*

Upstairs at Ca'n Manin there was the solar — a storeroom in the old days-now a second sitting-room but seldom used, and leading off that two bedrooms. In the solar were two worn easy chairs, a bookcase filled with paperbacks, a Mallorquin inlaid sideboard that had a vaguely Egyptian air about it, and four carpets, two Ispahans, a Gum and a Mir, which were the only things Elvina had brought out from her home in England and which clearly held a special sentimental value for her.

He crossed one carpet — Elvina fussed over them, personally cleaning them and never letting Catalina go near them — opened the french windows and stepped out on to the balcony. It had become a routine for him to spend some time looking at the scene before going to bed: it held so much peace. To the left, across the intervening six kilometres of land, was the moon-streaked bay, ringed by mountains, the nearer clearly visible, the more distant ones ghostlike as they merged into the night. In the foreground, a kilometre away, was a hill on which stood a monastery: a place of pilgrimage, to those who had the energy and the wind to climb the twisting track, because there was a shrine in which was a casket containing the hip bone of a local saint. To the right of that hill was a second one, Puig Llueso, on which, and around which, was the town of Llueso — a village, by local definition, even though over seven thousand people lived there. To the right again was the valley along which ran the road to Creyola and its famous monastery, and this valley was guarded by a mountain which looked like a giant's head, nose uppermost.

Peace, he thought, as a gentle breeze slid past his face, was something this island had to offer. Away from the beaches, the tourist traps, the frenetic conglomerations of hotels, cafes, bars, tea-rooms, curio shops, discotheques and night-clubs, the island seemed timeless. Elvina, divining his greatest need, had driven him to all her favourite places where the tourists seldom bothered to go: to woods where the air was heavy with the scent of pine and wild herbs, to the mountains where the terrain was moonlike, to the inland lanes where donkey carts rolled along the roads, their drivers snoozing.

Jennifer — and faced by the moonlit scene of peace he could think of her with regret yet with a growing resignation — would have loved the place. She'd always loved islands and the suggestion of a simpler life led on them.

He turned and went inside, shut the french windows, trod carefully and as little as possible on the carpets, and crossed to the back bedroom.

The weather, changing with the rapidity with which it so often did on a fairly mountainous island in the early part of the year, became sunny with not a cloud in the sky.

Tatham carried coffee, bread and marmalade on a tray out on to the patio. He ate beyond the balcony, where concrete pillars supported a grid of wire along which two vines, now shooting, were trained. Six feet below the patio — all the ground was sloping away from the mountain behind so that it was terraced-was the small garden in which was a ragged lawn, a circular, narrow fishpond with a tangerine tree growing in the centre, a surrounding bed of geraniums, two orange, one walnut and one pomegranate tree. Beyond and below the garden was an orange grove, almost a hectare in size. It was all very different from the garden at Sadacre Farm. Then he remembered the farm was no longer his. He wondered how the new tenant was making out and whether the lay in the four-acre field had taken well.

A car rounded the wall at the far corner of the next-door property — belonging to a wealthy American woman who, Elvina said, had become so Spanish she'd even changed her name to a Spanish one and refused to entertain either Americans or English, but whose proselytization had stopped short at shifting her capital out of the States. The car bounced up the dirt track, turned at the estanque, and parked next to the garage. A short man, with an egg-shaped, smiling face, a jaw heavily stubbled, and wearing rough clothes, climbed out and came up to the table where Tatham sat. He spoke rapidly in Spanish.

'I'm sorry,' Tatham replied, 'but I don't understand a word.'

This made the man speak even more quickly.

Elvina leaned out of the window of her bedroom. 'Who is it …? Oh, it's the landlord, José! What the hell's he doing here so early?'

José Mayans Bravo — like all Spaniards, he used his wife's maiden name as well as his own — looked up and smiled more broadly than ever and wished her a good morning. She replied forcefully and his smile became less. She then spoke to Tatham. 'Blast the man! I'd better come down and sort him out. Just can't take a hint.' She withdrew.

Any hint she'd given, thought Tatham, had been driven home with a verbal sledgehammer.

When she came out on to the patio, she was dressed in frayed dressing-gown, a pair of pyjamas, and a battered pair of slippers. 'Is there any coffee?'

He stood up. 'I'll go and make some fresh.' He carried the tray through to the kitchen and there refilled the Espresso machine and put it on the stove. The coffee made quickly and he took it out, together with cup, saucer, milk, and sugar. Elvina was sitting down on one of the metal garden chairs and was waving a forefinger at Mayans, who was looking sheepish.

'The bloody rogue: they're all rogues,' she said, in tones of affection. 'Put one within scenting distance of a peseta and he'd knife his own grandmother to get it. This is the third time in the past six months he's tried to get me to pay more rent. Says he's now having to support half a dozen relatives and is desperate for money. He knows perfectly well that I know he doesn't support anyone, not even his own wife.'

'Can he force you to pay more?'

'No!' She helped herself to milk and sugar, sipped the coffee, then added a little more sugar. 'When I came out here, this rascal offered me the place on a lifelong lease at a rent he thought was exorbitant and when I signed up he reckoned he'd made a hell of a good bargain. But I could see what was going to happen to prices and rents and I knew that in a year or two I'd be laughing. I am, now.' Mayans looked from one to the other of them, then spoke to her in a soft, pleading voice.

Elvina finished her coffee and replaced the cup on the saucer with a bang. '"Just a thousand a month more. It won't hurt the Señora and it'll save me from starving." As if one can't see that he's got a long, long way to go before he starves.'

'The poor man doesn't realize who he's up against.' Elvina laughed, to the evident annoyance of Mayans who spoke indignantly.

'Now he's getting on his high horse. Great chaps for dignity, out here. Says I won't treat him seriously. Of course I won't treat his cries of poverty seriously when he spends most of his spare time at the Llueso Club drinking brandy. It's easy to guess what's really irking him. They're all so sharp at business that they can't stand a despised foreigner getting the better of them … Still, I suppose we ought to take pity on him. Go and get the brandy, will you, please. We'll pour a couple of large tots down him and maybe he'll feel more cheerful.'

Brandy for breakfast, thought Tatham, as he walked into the house, was undoubtedly a great recipe for calming down an irate landlord.

CHAPTER IV

JUDY TOYNBEE said to her stepfather, 'I'll be off, then, Larry. See you some time this evening, if you're still up.'

'Sure,' Ingham replied.

'And don't forget to order some whisky: we're down to the last bottle.'

He watched her leave, a tall, slim woman, direct in manner, too direct, many said, with an attractive if petulant face which was slightly off-set so that her two profiles were distinctly dissimilar. She was spending the day with Will Brown. Will was a small-time crook, he thought patronizingly, dealing in cheap property illegally — under Spanish law he needed qualifications he did not possess — swindling his English clients in any one, or more, of several time-honoured ways. But Judy must know what kind of a man he was — all the residents did. She was quite possibly going out with him simply because of his reputation.

He crossed the very large sitting-room and stared out at the distant bay through the right-hand large picture window. Will Brown was lucky, he suddenly thought irrationally. He'd kept his feet on the ground and stayed with the small property market and so when things went wrong his losses didn't cripple him. But he, Lawrence Ingham, had had visions of grandeur and had started his own urbanization and had built also the house he now lived in, Ca'n Xema, to millionaires' standards. So when things went wrong, they went really wrong.

It was basically all the fault of the Spanish government. They'd been talking about levying rates and taxes for years, but no one had ever really expected them to implement their threats. But they had, including a thumping tax on undeveloped building sites. How many undeveloped building sites did he have on his urbanization? And then the Spanish government hadn't devalued the peseta when the pound and the dollar dropped to the floor and so prospective buyers of luxury houses became rarer than capitalists in China.

If he joined all his unpaid bills together, they'd stretch from where to where? Too bloody far.

The future wasn't as bleak as the present. It couldn't be. The pound and the dollar would appreciate against the peseta, money would return, the more expensive houses would sell. But how long before then and would he be around to see the change? The most conservative of estimates said that if he didn't soon find five million pesetas, he was finished.

It wasn't the first time he'd been short of money. Two of his three marriages had been undertaken as a result of financial difficulties. But that solution was probably no longer open to him. Every time he looked in a mirror he seemed to see deeper and more lines of dissipation, more grey hairs, and now he'd need a lot of luck to grab a wealthy widow: or else she'd be so old that he couldn't go through with it.

He lit a cigarette: American, smuggled. He never did anything cheaply, not even when he hardly dared step into any one of the three banks he dealt with. All his houses were built of the best materials, despite the attempts of the local builders to substitute the cheapest. He drove a Mercedes shooting-brake on French plates (which meant he paid no tax on it). His suits were made in London and now cost over two hundred guineas each. If Judy needed a new frock, he gave her a cheque for ten or fifteen thousand pesetas and told her to buy a small French number in Palma.

He was in trouble because he needed five million pesetas. Not so long ago, before he'd become ambitious, he could have found five million with little trouble. But he'd become big business and so, ironically, the availability of cash had become very much less. If he sold up everything that was easily and readily saleable, he couldn't realize more than two and a half million. And he daren't try to make more by selling cheaply, because people would know he was in trouble and they'd be snapping all around him like an army of sharks.

He turned away from the window. The sitting-room, he thought, was the most attractive room he'd ever designed. The proportions were exactly right. The ceiling was high and beamed, the marble fireplace baronial but not exaggerated, the high-quality reproduction furniture went perfectly with the hand-painted tiles, the two tapestries were genuine if minor Gobelin (smuggled across the border in his car), the built-in bookcase was filled with matched leather-bound books that could improve any man's mind, even a rich man's. Beyond were dining-room, music-room, breakfast-room, study, five principal bedrooms and bathrooms all en suite and all with doors carved to traditional Spanish patterns, an upstairs sitting-room, together with very full domestic quarters, to use the professional jargon, servants' quarters, and even two further bedrooms for the poor relations. A home for a millionaire ... or Herr Naupert. He crossed to the middle of three doors and opened it to show a small but well-stocked bar. He poured himself out a Campari, vermouth, and soda.

Naupert was a hard bastard, he thought with irritated admiration. No wonder he was reputedly one of the richest industrialists in Germany. He'd first lined up Naupert a year ago. Very rich, an art collector and amateur art critic of standing, looking for a place in the sun because this had become the thing for a rich German businessman to have even if he was too busy making money ever to use it. A natural mark for an ambitious property seller. He'd travelled to Germany and made casual contact — that had cost him a fistful of marks — and after spending a lot more money on entertaining Naupert had casually let it be known he had a beautiful house in the most beautiful part of Mallorca which he might be persuaded to sell to someone he really liked who appreciated it. Naupert had said, with brutal directness, that now one question was answered because he'd been wondering from the beginning what Herr Ingham was selling. That night, Ingham had for the first time thought he might be getting a bit old for the racket.

However, Naupert had finally agreed he did want to buy a house in Mallorca. Ingham flew him and his wife out to the island, first class, VIP treatment all the way, and showed him the house — Ca'n Xema had not then been quite completed. The Nauperts had looked over it and after a further six expensive days at the Hotel Parelona — Ingham paying — had said no, it wasn't quite what they wanted and in any case it was priced at a million and a half pesetas too much. Ingham still didn't know which of the many English bastards in Llueso had betrayed him and leaked to the Nauperts the reasonable price for the house.

He'd crossed the Nauperts off his list because you couldn't do profitable business with people who refused to let their wallets be dictated to by their hearts. But then the money shortage had become very bad and it was essential to sell Ca'n Xema and the Nauperts were the only people he could think of who were likely to be able to afford such a place.

Why hadn't they bought the first house? If he could find the answer to this, he might be able to sell them Ca'n Xema. The million and a half pesetas couldn't be the reason. A hard-headed bastard of a German businessman would have been delighted to bargain away this extra. No, they just hadn't liked the house (it was difficult to judge what influence his wife had had on his decision because she hardly ever spoke). Why hadn't they liked it? And the only answer he had come to, reluctantly because he could so easily be wrong, was that it just hadn't been expensive enough. Naupert might appear the very epitome of rock-hard sensibility, but he could be subject to ordinary human emotions, including that of wanting it to be clear, without making it clear, that he didn't keep up with the Joneses, he was the de Hartville-Smiths. The first house had been very attractive, in a beautiful position, and expensive, but it was possible to name three other houses in the area as good. Owning that house, the Nauperts would have been remarked, but not remarkable. But Ca'n Xema was unique. On a perfect site, its only disadvantage being close to the mountain so that the sun was lost by four in the afternoon, it was built with drystone walls which alone marked it out amongst all others. Then the overall design had all the pleasing warmth of classical simplicity, unspoilt by any hint of baroque extravagance — in contrast to too many of the larger houses which looked as though they'd been designed by left-handed, fumble-fisted plumbers with delusions of grandeur — and the landscaped, terraced garden couldn't be matched by anyone other than the Eastmores. The owner of Ca'n Xema must unmistakably be very rich and very successful. Which was why the Nauperts would buy it, if they ever did.

Just showing them the house and quoting a price wasn't going to be enough. Forget the wife. Naupert suffered from pride, but he was also a very keen businessman and when it came to buying this house those two factors were going to join battle. Ca'n Xema would bolster his pride, but empty his pocket. So which way would he jump? Reluctantly, Ingham had previously decided that the businessman would win through and that, failing anything else, Naupert would not buy Ca'n Xema. Which was why, three months ago, he'd telephoned Antonio Galan in Ibiza, arranged a meeting in Palma at the Hotel Obispo, and there commissioned Galan to paint a Renoir which he was going to present to Naupert as a poor fake.

CHAPTER V

THE ENGLISH COMMUNITY at Llueso and Puerto Llueso numbered about four hundred and the English Community about two hundred. The subtle difference between the two was a source of much pride, heart-burning, and jealousy amongst the English and mystification amongst the foreigners — particularly the Americans who really did believe that one man was as good as another if each was worth the same number of dollars.

The English Community prided itself on upholding old-fashioned — and none the worse for that — standards. Breeding and manners were clearly far more important than mere wealth although, of course, sufficient wealth did help a person to overcome his or her background provided he or she was not a pop star, married to a native (in this sense, a Mallorquin or a Spaniard without aristocratic ancestry), engaged in trade on the island (here, the classifications became far too obscure for any foreigner to follow), or a writer who hadn't won a Nobel prize.

Breeding was a matter of record and manners were self-evident, but wealth could only be proved in the most subtle manner: to be nouveau riche was automatically to be Non-C (Non-Community). To be clever was almost as fatal.

In order to maintain its ethos and to meet every member's need for a Queen-like figure, a cross between a friendly white Protestant God and Emily Post, it was necessary to have a leader. Their leader was Lady Mary Eastmore.

A Frenchman would have described her, if forced to do so, as *formidable*. She was approaching sixty, though not too quickly, and her skin had the dried-up, used look, despite all the care lavished on it, which came from many years spent in the tropics. Her face was long with a square and decided chin, her mouth was on the firm side, and her eyes were light blue and icy. Her hair was nut-brown, turning grey. Her body was on the thin side and her breasts were satisfactorily small — she disliked breasts. Her voice was in keeping — high-pitched, loud, drawlingly accented, and at times infuriating. The natives in one of the colonies where she'd been the governor's wife had christened her 'The

29

macaw with a twisted tongue'. She was always correct and polite, especially to those to whom it was not strictly necessary, and she never lost her temper.

She believed it to be the divine right of certain few people to be the leaders and of the rest to be the led, and in the monarchy. On the Queen's birthdays, actual and official, she personally hoisted the Union Jack to the top of the flagpole in the centre of the lawn.

She possessed breeding and untainted wealth. Her husband's title went all the way back to Charles the Second and a rather unrefined mistress and his wealth came largely from the middle of the nineteenth century (sweated labour in factories) which was far enough back to remove the slightest taint of trade.

An American who'd been subjected to a lecture on the disastrous effect on the world of the antagonistic American ignorance of enlightened colonial rule had called her a stupid old bitch. Bitch she might be, stupid she was not. She had read *Don Quijote de la Mancha* in the original and not many Spaniards ever kept going to the end of that endless book. She knew some of Miguel Llobera's poems by heart, which few Mallorquins did. She had corrected the visiting Anglican bishop on his rendering of Proverbs XXIII 31, pointing out that no matter what the revised edition of the Bible stated, the noted Jewish scholar, Shlomo Washftig, had recently cast doubts — which seemed to have good grounds — on the generally accepted translation. She knew the rules of precedence backwards and could, without a second's thought, correctly seat at the dinner table the Iranian foreign minister, a minor prince of one of the Gulf sheikdoms, an Australian mining millionaire unconnected with Poseidon, the cousin of one of the Queen's ladies-in-waiting, the elder son of an earl who'd renounced his title, and a prebendary who was a pederast.

She was at work at her Louis XVI bureau in the study when the butler knocked and entered. She looked up, momentarily annoyed that even after three years Miguel failed to understand that he should not knock before entering any of the public rooms.

'The people with the flowers have arrived, my lady,' he said in Spanish, except for the two words 'my lady' which she insisted he spoke in English. He pronounced them, 'me laydi'.

'Are they exactly what I ordered?'

'Exactly as you …'

'Have you personally checked them?'

He gesticulated with his hands. 'Everything.'

'Have the canapés arrived?'

'I am waiting now for the airport to phone to say they have arrived, my lady.'

'That won't be of much use, will it? Surely you know your own country and countrymen?'

'I am Spanish, my lady, not Mallorquin,' he said lugubriously.

'Good heavens, do you think I've time to be concerned about that sort of detail? Get on to the airport immediately, find out if the canapés have arrived, speak to the Customs and say the goods are not subject to tax whatever they think, and if they want to argue, refer them to Senor Cifre and demand to know why they haven't notified us by phone as instructed to do so.'

There was a scratching on the door. 'Let Fru-Fru in,' she ordered.

Miguel opened the door and Fru-Fru, daughter of Show Champion Tso-Ch'iao and of Show Champion Hui Tying, a Shih Tzu of breeding even more impeccably pure than her mistress's, padded into the room, jumped up on to her lap, and settled down. She stroked the dog's ears. 'Very well, that's all,' she said. 'But you're to ring the airport immediately.'

Miguel left. As he passed through the sitting-room he saw that the day remained cloudless and it seemed certain it would be fine for the evening reception and he felt a bewildered resentment that God should be so magnanimous towards heretics.

Lady Eastmore returned to her work, checking the household accounts to make certain the servants did not make more than a few pesetas' commission from the shops at which they bought the food and drink. She was interrupted twenty minutes later when her husband came in. 'It's time for a drink, dear,' he said. 'What would you like?'

'I'll have my usual half bottle of champagne, please, Charles.'

'And I think I'll have a scotch.' He picked up the internal phone on the desk and ordered the two drinks. He was a tall, well-built man, with the kind of battered handsome face which inspired confidence. He had grey hair, greying eyebrows, and a grey moustache. He possessed the same air of self-confident authority as his wife, but in his case this was mellowed by an obvious affability. He'd been a good governor in the far-flung colonies to which he'd been called and although his portrait in oils had, along with other portraits of other governors, often been taken down and burned in public demonstrations after independence, he was still remembered by some with respect and even affection.

She looked up. 'I told you Norah is coming to stay with us very soon, didn't I?'

'Yes,' he answered, as he sat down.

Her expression sharpened. 'Norah is a very old friend of the family.'

'Of course, dear.'

She decided not to pursue the matter. 'I've also heard from Laura today that she doesn't think she'll be able to come out in late May.'

'I'm very sorry to hear that,' he said with genuine regret. 'What's the trouble?'

'Her father's been taken rather ill and it looks nasty.'

'Poor old boy. And it's only a little more than a year ago when he and I were shooting together at Donald's. Damned good shot, he is. There was an old cock which came corkscrewing over ...'

'Quite. I think I shall write to Marion and see if she's free to come instead.'

That was a pity, he thought, but made no comment. Their lives had long since fallen into a pattern which both recognized and usually respected — Norah tended to be an exception — without a word on the subject having been spoken. She invited whom she wished and he was polite to them: he invited whom he wished and she in turn was polite to them.

'Angela is engaged to a boy in the Guards,' she went on. 'Marion says he's a bit of a weed, but in this day and age one has to be thankful he's at least doing something respectable. Did I tell you that Marion's son, Basil, has been arrested and charged with smoking marijuana?'

'Basil? Good God! It's quite incredible.' It was quite incredible to both of them. They had been brought up to observe strict rules of behaviour and had always done so. When she'd been told by specialists that she could never bear any children and so in consequence she had stopped all sex, having a keen sense of the ridiculous, he had accepted her decision with fortitude and without recriminations. His subsequent liaisons had always been conducted with the greatest discretion.

'Of course, Marion has never had enough backbone where those children of hers are concerned. I can remember when Basil was having a sordid affair with some sort of model and all Marion could do was worry about whether he would catch a nasty disease.'

That always was a bit of a problem, he thought.

There was a knock on the door and Miguel came in with a silver salver on which were a whisky glass with a scotch on the rocks, a tulip-shaped champagne glass, and a half bottle of champagne in a silver bucket. Lady Eastmore thought about telling Miguel not to knock, then sighed: they should have imported a proper butler from England. Miguel opened the champagne and poured out a glassful, allowing it to foam too much, put the bucket by the side of her desk, and handed them both their drinks. He left, no word having been spoken.

'By the way, Mary,' said Lord Eastmore, as the door shut, 'I'm off after lunch for a round of golf with Paddy.'

'You won't be late back, will you?' She sipped her champagne.

He smiled, showing even, white teeth. 'As if on today of all days I'd dare!'

She smiled back at him. They respected each other and enjoyed each other's company, so could usually joke about their existing relationship. 'By the way, Alice told me something about Paddy yesterday which I hope isn't true.'

'That Andrew's gone to live with him? Paddy told me so himself the other day. I'm surprised it's taken Alice so long to catch up with the news.'

'It's very blatant, isn't it?'

He shrugged his shoulders. 'It's none of my business. And Paddy plays a damned good game of golf.'

'In the old days, no one would have received him any more.'

'If we stopped receiving anyone whose morals aren't what they ought to be, we'd lead a lonely life out here.'

'That's being very cynical, Charles. Most people know how to behave.' She pursed her lips. She and he never agreed over matters sexual. Not that, in this case, she was really complaining about the fact that Paddy was a homosexual — many of her friends in England were homosexuals. But it simply was not done to publish so blatantly one's aberrations. 'I do hope Paddy doesn't bring Andrew with him tonight.'

'I expect he will.'

She sighed. 'They make life so difficult. As if we didn't have enough trouble, with people like Elvina around.'

'Don't tell me she's living with another woman?'

She had to laugh. 'You're quite impossible, Charles. You know very well what I meant. Elvina is one of those women who go out of their way to be impossibly difficult. I'm quite certain she'll wear one of those awful old frocks of hers that looks as if she's on her way to go charring. And why can't she at least have her hair cut properly? It would make her look a shade less barbaric.'

'Perhaps she won't come.'

'She'll come simply because she knows how much her presence annoys me.'

'Then why do you ask her?'

She didn't reply. In any case, he knew the answer. Duty. These annual receptions were the equivalent of the old governor's parties they'd had to give. To them had been invited all manner of people who were not invited at any other time of the year — especially as independence had drawn near — in order to show the flag: it had been a service she'd undertaken because it had been her duty. And, of course, there'd always been someone like Elvina to let the side down. But by asking such people the act of service became that much more difficult, and the more difficult it was, the greater the duty one had nobly carried out. Even the Elvinas of the world had their uses.

'I've heard something a bit disturbing,' he said. 'There's some sort of official from the Bank of England over here at the moment, snooping around for illegal bank accounts, houses bought without the bank's permission or the dollar premium being paid, capital illicitly brought out … All that sort of thing.'

'He'll be very busy, then.'

'Quite so.' Indeed, the man would be, if he learned even a tenth of what had gone on over the past years.

*

The square in Llueso, bounded by plane trees and, on three sides, by roads, was on a slope and so the south end had been built up in order to keep it level: at the south end, there was a small fountain and flower-beds. Here, the vegetable and fish markets were held every Sunday, fairs were pitched, fiestas began or ended, bonfires were lit, rockets were fired without regard to where the spent cases would land, the town band gave concerts, and important visitors were received by the mayor. To the north-west lay the church, tall and rather severe on the outside, opulent and colourful on the inside. To the south-east was the Llueso Club, theoretically open to women yet by tradition not so. Two banks overlooked the square, two cafés pitched tables and chairs on it. The offices of the Municipal Police were down a turning off it, while the post office, telephone exchange and telegraph office were all within two minutes' walk of it. From it in one direction one could just see the top of the hill, Puig Llueso, on which was a small shrine and a figure of Christ on the Cross; in the other direction was visible the monastery on the top of its hill.

José Mayans sat at one of the tables in the bar of the Llueso Club, drinking a brandy and wondering how long before he must make a move and return to his wife's shop in the Puerto and do some sort of work. Not very long. Marie watched the clock as if she were a factory inspector. And if he were too long, on his return she'd give him hell even if the shop were filled with tourists. She had a tongue like a Toledo blade. By tradition, the Mallorquin wife was subserviently obedient, but Marie was no traditionalist. It was, he thought morosely, all the tourists' fault. Before tourism had so altered the island, even a woman like Marie would have known and kept her place.

A loud, boisterous voice disturbed his gloomy thoughts. 'So what's up with you? Received an invitation to your own funeral?'

He looked up. Jiménez, large, tubby, oozing bonhomie, grinned down at him.

'Come on, man, if it's that bad, cut your throat and leave the rest of us to have a laugh.'

'What's got you all excited?' demanded Mayans in a disgruntled tone of voice.

'I have just sold three thousand square metres of useless, rocky land to a Frenchman for a million. One million pesetas.'

'If you'd waited, you'd have got two million.'

Jiménez sat down on a rocky wooden chair. He thumped the wooden table with his huge fist and Mayans's glass jiggled and the brandy surged around it. 'You're sourer than an October orange. D'you know, if you won the lottery, I'll swear you'd burst into tears. What's the matter? Has Marie been giving you hell again?' He roared with laughter.

If only, thought Mayans, he didn't have the misfortune to be married to a wife who'd inherited fincas and land and who was so good a businesswoman she was making a fortune out of the curio and antique shop. It made her think she was smart. Smart enough to tell him she wasn't keeping him and he ought to get a job.

'You know something?' Jiménez's mouth expressed salacious enjoyment. 'You should eat plenty of oysters and drink a lot of Binissalem wine and then perhaps your little palm tree would grow enough to give Marie a big belly to keep her busy with women's work.'

'There's nothing wrong with me,' he protested.

'Then why no children? Me — I have five and any night now we start on the sixth.' He roared with laughter, turned, and shouted to the waiter for two Fundadors. 'Perhaps you drink too much cognac? Cognac is bad for it. Perhaps you smoke too much? Smoking is bad for it.'

'All right. Everything's bad for it.'

'Not everything. Work is excellent for it. But maybe Marie still does all the work for the both of you.' He slapped Mayans on the back and Mayans hit his stomach on the edge of the table.

The big fat Moorish bastard, thought Mayans, as he rubbed his stomach. 'I've got to go.'

'With drinks arriving? What are you? A Madrid tailor?' The waiter brought the drinks. 'Phone his wife,' said Jiménez to the waiter, 'and tell her he's not feeling very well and can't return until he's had a lie-down.'

'That's the excuse I used last time,' replied the waiter, 'and she didn't believe me then.' He returned to the bar.

Jiménez raised his glass and drank the contents straight down. 'That's better. It doesn't do a stomach good to be without food for very long.' He leaned forward. 'You haven't said what's troubling you? Has Marie missed a couple of mil notes from the till?'

'D'you think she doesn't watch the till closer than that?' Mayans answered bitterly. 'And if she's not watching it, that girl she's taken on is.'

'So now you've a girl in the place? Maybe you've …?'

'Of course not.'

'Your Marie watches everything too closely, eh?'

Jiménez called for two more cognacs. 'Tell me, José, how is business? I don't mean the shop. We all know Marie makes a fortune there. I mean the real business, the property, the millionaire's business?' He rubbed forefinger and thumb together in a universally expressive gesture.

'All right,' replied Mayans sulkily.

'When you told us a long time ago — longer than I care to remember because a man gets old quickly — that you were going to manage all Marie's business for her, I said to Ernesto, there walks a man who is so clever he soon will be rich enough to buy the whole of this end of the island.'

Laugh your head off, thought Mayans sourly.

'And wasn't I right? Within a month, the big deal. You let a finca to a rich Englishwoman at a rent even a Palma robber would respect.'

'I must go.' Mayans stood up.

'Sit down,' said Jiménez, as he kicked the other's feet from under him so that Mayans sat with a thump that jarred his spine. 'In only a month, the very big deal. A month! No one but a great businessman could act that fast. But you were so modest about it all.'

The waiter arrived at the table with two more glasses of brandy.

'D'you remember,' said Jiménez to the waiter, 'how modest José was about his incredible success at the property business?'

'Sure,' replied the waiter. 'No boasting at all. Even confessed it might take him half a year to make enough to retire and buy a manor house and employ half a dozen servants.' He put the glasses down on the table, picked up the empty ones, and left.

Jiménez drank his second brandy as quickly as his first. He wiped his mouth with the back of a hairy hand. 'But Marie, she got jealous. Just like a woman. Can't stand a man being a very big success. She didn't want you any longer in the property business in case you did everything for her. Eh?' Jiménez dug his elbow in Mayans's side, causing Mayans to slop brandy over his clothes.

Jiménez was a child, torturing a poor joke to death, thought Mayans. And had Jiménez been so clever in his life? He didn't own a manor house or, for that much, even a respectable finca. He hadn't foreseen the incredible rise in rents and house prices that was to come. So it had been a mistake to agree a lifelong rent for the unfurnished finca. But if it hadn't been for the rise in all the prices, that rent would have been a clever one. And he wasn't the only person in Llueso to have guessed wrongly.

'I think, though, that perhaps the Englishwoman must also be clever?' said Jiménez, his huge head tilted to one side, malicious amusement gleaming in his dark eyes. 'Because perhaps in the end she had a little better bargain than you did?'

Mayans finished his brandy. 'She's made many improvements which she's paid for, but which now belong to the house,' he said weakly.

'I knew it! You've been a genius all along, no matter what it's looked like to ignorant people like myself. She doesn't pay a full rent, but she turns your house into a palace for you. Has she put gold on the taps and lined the floors with Italian marble?' He turned and shouted to the waiter. 'Two more cognacs to celebrate.'

Mayans stood up and hastily stepped out of range.

'So you have to rush to do more profitable business? Letting other houses at little rent so the rich foreigners rebuild them for you?'

Mayans left the building and his only consolation was that he hadn't paid for any of the drinks, not even the couple before Jiménez had entered.

He walked down a small side street to his car, parked away from the club in case someone reported its presence there to Marie. He sat down behind the wheel and lit a cigarette. Just because an ugly old foreign woman had been lucky, he was laughed at by everyone and treated with contempt by his wife. One day, he'd show the lot of 'em.

CHAPTER VI

THE EASTMORES' HOUSE was in La Huerta de Llueso. It was an attractive ranch-style bungalow, built on piles to avoid rising damp, large enough to be discreetly imposing, but not so large as to be vulgar. The garden was terraced, since it lay on the dying slopes of the mountain behind, and a full-time gardener kept it in perfect order and as near to a traditional English garden as one could get with bougainvillaea, poinsettias, palm trees, loquats, persimmons, oranges, prickly pear cacti, and century plants everywhere. The oval swimming pool, in the centre of a lawn of the local creeping grass which felt like corrugated cardboard to walk on, was on the same level as the house and to the right of it. Round the pool had been built a complex of bar, dining area, terrace, kitchen, barbecue pit, changing rooms, and lavatory. In each of the changing rooms was a discreet notice in English which said: 'Please observe the proprieties before swimming.' To the north of the house was a circular drive, closely modelled on the huge circular drive of the country home they had sold many years ago, and in the centre of this was a flower-bed always filled with annuals in flower.

When there was a reception, the field to the east of the house was opened up and all the cars were parked there. Lady Eastmore employed two full-time maids and they, together with two friends brought in for the evening, wore matching striped cotton frocks, lace-edged pinafores, and lace caps on their heads. They handed round the drinks, but food was served from long tables in the pool complex because Lady Eastmore disliked bits and pieces being dropped everywhere. Champagne — French, naturally — was offered to everyone, but those without the taste to enjoy this could ask for anything else except beer.

Decorations were standard and traditional. Coloured lights from Harrods were looped through the trees, out-of-season flowers in pots were set around the pool, thousands of rose petals were floated on the floodlit pool, and the Union Jack was hoisted on the flag-pole and illuminated.

Elvina and Tatham, Elvina driving her Fiat, arrived late, even by Mallorquin standards. The gardener, wearing a peaked cap with proud self-consciousness, directed them where to park and Elvina parked elsewhere. She climbed out and loudly demanded to know from the gardener when he was going to let her have that white poinsettia? The gardener replied that the señora must not be in a hurry, it would occur one day. He came much closer and lowered his voice in conspiratorial manner. The señor and the señora of the house were said to be going away on holiday later in the year and perhaps the white poinsettia would arrive in the señora's garden at around that time.

As they walked out of the field, Tatham said accusingly: 'Great Aunt Elvina, you've been arranging to swipe that plant.'

'Of course,' she answered, with composure. 'I've always wanted a white one and the local garden shop had five last year, but by the time I learned about them, Mary had bought all five. She should have the manners to leave some for others.'

They went through the gateway — wrought-iron gates bearing the Eastmore crest were hung on flanking, curved brick walls — and along the path past the house to the pool, the lawn, the coloured lights, the out-of-season flowers, the floating rose petals, and the one hundred and ninety-two other guests.

Elvina, wearing a shabby cotton frock she had chosen with care, introduced Lady Eastmore to Tatham. Hearing he came from Kent, she asked him if he were related to the Tathams of Great Stour Hall and when he said he wasn't she smiled briefly and commiseratingly, murmured a hope he would enjoy himself, and turned to speak to someone else.

A maid came up with a tray of champagne and Elvina and Tatham each took a glass. Elvina introduced Tatham to the maid, shook hands to the evident surprise of a nearby couple, asked how her family was and in particular her young sister. The maid, animated for the first time that evening, said her younger sister was now very much better after that terrible accident and it was very kind of the señora to ask.

'You obviously get on well with the Mallorquins,' said Tatham, after the maid had left them.

'Of course. Provided you're not trying to do business with them, they're charming. And Francisca, the maid, is a special case. She's worked to death here — none of them can stand up to Mary — and then her father demands all the money she makes and spends it on buying rubbish like television and three-piece suites and all the other things we've taught them to hold worthwhile. It's a tragedy — though no one can see it. This island may have known poverty before the tourists came, but the Mallorquins had a natural dignity and they'd got their values right. Then the tourists arrived in their millions and the poverty vanished, but all the values of the people became twisted and perverted ... But don't listen to me. I'm an old woman crookedly looking back in time. Anything's better than poverty — even television.'

'Do many people see things as you do?'

'Not many. All the English are concerned about is inflation and the devalued pound. Beyond that, they can't think.' He laughed.

'It's true. They're all running away from something — taxes, neighbours, memories, suburbia, socialism — and if they think too hard, they begin to remember.'

He was running away, if only temporarily. From Jennifer's death. Yet this island was giving him the peace even to remember that without too much hurt.

'When I first came, I was running away from Paul's death,' she said, as if consciously carrying forward his thoughts. 'But eventually I wasn't any longer and it became my real home. I like to think I belong here, unlike them.' She swept her hand round in a semi-circle. 'I don't keep demanding efficiency and trying to import other countries' values and goods. I like the values here: inefficiency and shoddy workmanship, true, but smiles, friendship, laughter, an enjoyment of life ... You see, I am as stupid and as perverse as people say I am. A moment ago I was bewailing the advent of twisted values, now I'm saying the old values still exist. Never mind. If you can't be stupid and perverse at my age, when can you be? But never make the mistake of thinking it's a place for someone of your age to come to live in. It's a lotus island, suffocating enthusiasm, ambition, opposition ... Everything the young should know and enjoy.' She drained her glass.

A man of medium height, hair too curly to be entirely natural, monogram on open-necked green silk shirt, lavender linen trousers with knife-edged creases, walked up to them. 'Elvina, dear lady, what an unexpected pleasure! I thought you never, but never, came to these simply ghastly receptions, but sat at home and cast spells? What have you been doing with yourself recently? ... if that's not a rude question.' He tilted his head to one side.

'That's none of your business,' she said briskly, her manner totally different from what it had been a moment before.

'I do adore the way you say exactly what you think: everyone else is so circumambulatory. By the way, have you heard about Mavis?'

'Whatever's that silly woman been up to now?'

'She's gone off with the young man from the garage — that divine blond Apollo.'

'You sound jealous?'

'That's very horrid of you. In future, I shan't tell you all the interesting news. Who's your lovely friend?'

'Someone whom I was hoping not to have to introduce you to. John, this is Barry. John's my great-nephew.'

'Lovely meeting you, John. I do hope you've come to live amongst us?'

'I'm only here for a short stay,' replied Tatham. 'Elvina's very kindly putting me up.'

'Wonderful! I want you to know that Elvina is one of my dearest friends. So refreshingly different. So delightfully direct. Talking to her is like a walk on the moors in a gale.'

'You're damn glad when it's over,' said Elvina drily.

'Now, now. You're much too sharp. I shall talk to your great-nephew — makes it sound as if he's ten foot tall, doesn't it? — who looks so much kinder. How do you like our island, John?'

'It's very lovely.'

'Ah! Betrayed out of your own mouth as a tourist. You should know that in reality this is a positive sink of iniquity: a twentieth-century Sodom and Gomorrah.'

'I was referring to the scenery,' said Tatham amusedly, 'not the morals.'

'That! But that's pure chocolate-box. You can't be serious — you can't possibly like all those horrid rocks and mountains? You really ought to talk to our poor little Penelope — that Amazon over there with such lovely billowy boobies — who paints the scenery and makes it all look like Brighton in a snowstorm. But then she suffers from bilious attacks.'

Judy, dressed in a very smart and eye-catching trouser suit, pushed past a group of people and came up to them. 'Hallo, all.' She wore little make-up and her jet black hair was loose.

'Judy,' exclaimed Barry, 'you look simply divine! I just adore those trousers.'

'That's fine, so long as you go on adoring them from a distance.'

'But why so bitchy? Haven't we had enough champagne to mellow us?'

'A couple of cases wouldn't be enough to overcome this company,' she snapped.

'The company? But that's charming because it never changes. We all know everything interesting about everybody and there's no room for surprises. I just hate surprises.'

'I heard you had one last week you didn't like at all.'

He looked momentarily disconcerted. 'You're being more than bitchy: you're being positively catty. I can't stay or I shall get a terrible headache. And I was having such a pleasant chat with Elvina and John who are the only intelligent people here.' He left.

Judy said abruptly: 'Sorry if I spoiled things, Elvina.'

'Don't be so silly. You know Barry. He only came to find out who John was and whether I'd taken on a gigolo. And now, after all that, you'd better meet John. My great-nephew from the side of the family I like.'

'Hallo,' she said offhandedly. 'It's the first time I knew Elvina liked any side of her family.' She studied him. 'So what dragged you along to this bun-fight?'

'It was Elvina's promise that I'd meet some charming people,' he answered.

Elvina laughed loudly. Judy's expression became a shade more sullen. 'All right. Barry was right. I'm in a bitchy mood.'

'Dare one ask why?'

'No reason. It's just there's nothing to do but drink and bitch. What are you doing out here? Taking a break from the City to observe with disdain the exiles at play?'

'I'm on a short holiday, but not from the City, and not with disdain.'

'His fiancée was killed in rather a nasty manner,' said Elvina with sharp belligerence. 'Very sensibly, he asked to come and stay with me to get away from everything. And I hope he's going to stay a long time … There's Winnie and I must have a word with her.' She left suddenly.

A maid came up to them with a tray of filled champagne glasses. Both of them changed an empty glass for a filled one.

'Would you have an English cigarette on you?' asked Judy, and her voice had lost its stridency.

He offered her a pack of Embassy.

'All right, I've made an obnoxious fool of myself and I'm sorry,' she said.

He flicked open his lighter. 'You weren't to know. Besides, it's beginning to seem like a long time ago.'

'But I could have minded my own business.'

'According to Elvina, that's the only thing that's never done here.'

'I guess she's about right. But then we must talk about something.'

He sipped his champagne. 'You sound as though you don't like being out here?'

'Like everyone else, I have a love-hate relationship with the place.'

'And with the people?'

She laughed and the lines of discontent vanished. 'You just have to be a newcomer to ask a question like that. We all dislike each other for various good reasons, but as there's no one else around we have to put up with people as they are. In any case, if one's referring to the people at this party, they're not my usual company. I'm certainly not Mary's idea of what a nice young lady should be.'

'What's she got against you?'

She studied him over the top of her glass. 'For a pleasant, uncontaminated newcomer from England, you're not doing too badly at being inquisitive …! In the first place, she's quite certain my stepfather will one day do something quite unforgivable which will naturally blacken everyone in the family. In the second, I've never left her in any doubt that I don't give a twopenny damn whether she leaves her visiting card, or not.'

'Her visiting card?'

'Surely you know this is the last remaining outpost of the British Empire where civilized standards of behaviour are strictly observed? She has visiting cards — engraved in England — and at the beginning of every year she leaves one of these on each family she will be graciously pleased to receive for the forthcoming three hundred and sixty-four days. Not to receive a card is the social kiss of death. One woman committed suicide on the second of January because she had received no visiting card — in fact, the maid had burned it.'

He smiled.

'You don't believe me?'

'Not a word. You're totally prejudiced and enjoying yourself trying to make a fool of me.'

'All right, you ask Elvina why the Portlands left this end of the island. Dear Mary caught him pinching one of her maid's bottoms at one of her intimate cocktail parties — he always did tend to take things literally. They were struck off the visiting list and, recognizing their utter disgrace, they scuttled away in the night.'

'No doubt to do public penance?'

'Maybe.'

'If you dislike your hostess that much, why come tonight?'

'She imports the smoked salmon direct from Scotland. I'll sell my soul any day of the week for Scotch smoked salmon.'

'And have you had some?'

'Not yet.'

'Then suppose we go in search of it?'

'Are you saying you'll go with me? Wouldn't you rather have sweeter company? There's Helen, over there, who'll never be rude about anyone or anything.'

He saw the woman Judy indicated. 'Perhaps. But neither will she get Paris ever to proposition her.'

'Now that showed a bitchy sense of humour which makes me look at you in a fresh and more favourable light. Come on, then, let's fight our way through to the smoked salmon. You can ask for four portions and with luck we'll get enough for two.'

'And you'll have my share?'

'You catch on fast.' She led the way through the swirling crowd of people, past the floodlit, rose-petalled swimming pool and the out-of-season pot plants, to the dining area in the pool complex where the food was set out on several tables.

*

Tatham drove Elvina's Fiat 128 the three kilometres into Llueso and parked in the square. He climbed out and looked up as a small flock of pigeons, alarmed by something, flew with a clatter of wings and were outlined first against the mountains and then the blue sky. It was a picture-postcard scene of quiet, lazy, sleepy peace. Yet Elvina said the Mallorquins had explosive tempers which could suddenly shatter the deepest peace. And during the Civil War there had been times of barbarous brutality: men dragged from their homes and taken up into the quiet, brooding mountains and shot because they had professed some sympathy with the Republicans, or they were owed money by those who shot, or they owned possessions which others wanted. Deep down, human nature didn't change, whether on a dreamy Mediterranean island or an English high street.

He walked from the square to the post-office and asked the man behind the counter, in one of the two Spanish phrases he had mastered, if there were any mail for Ca'n Manin. The man, smiling with pleasure because Tatham had bothered to try to speak Spanish, gave him four letters: one of these was for him from his mother. He returned to the car, sat down, and read the letter. His father had just sold a painting for more money than ever before, so they'd celebrated with a wonderful meal at the White Feathers. He smiled. His father believed money had only one use, spending. Within a couple of weeks, he'd be as short of money as ever and completely untroubled by the fact, while his mother would somehow manage. The letter finished up by saying that Mrs Payne had had to go into hospital for an operation.

Jennifer's mother had been complaining of bad health for some time, he remembered: the operation might prove a serious one. He visualized her as he had last seen her at the funeral and then he tried to visualize Jennifer, but he gained only a general impression without specific features, like an image from a dream. What would Jennifer have said about his spending so much of the previous evening with Judy? Had he been wrong to do so? But that was clearly being ridiculous. His grief at Jennifer's death was no less sincere because he had enjoyed talking to the black-haired, cynically amusing Judy.

He started the engine, backed out, turned, and drove out on to the Palma road rather than risk going through the back streets of Llueso which, narrow and without pavements, were totally unadapted to modern traffic needs.

Back at the house he handed Elvina her three letters and she suggested he pour out drinks for them. When he returned to the sitting-room and sat down, immediately under the large wrought-iron chandelier, she laid down the letter she'd been reading and looked at him and seemed about to speak, but finally did not and returned to reading the letter.

He drank, lit a cigarette, and stared through the window beyond the dining-recess. A greenfinch sat on the windowsill and pecked at the bird seed she put out each morning. After a while, probably with crop full to bursting, it flew off and sat in the branches of a plum tree. He picked up the book of wild flowers of South-West Europe and leafed through it, noting with surprise how many varieties Elvina had found — by each flower discovered on the island was written the exact spot and date. She loved to portray herself as a crabby old widow, he thought, but she had far too many interests in life for her ever to be that. She drove all over the island, seeking fresh species of flowers, and at the moment was in correspondence with the authors of this book over a plant which she had seen and which might be an entirely new species. She had a great interest in archaeology and studied many of the artefacts found in the talayots. She had carried out a one-woman census on the black vulture population of the eastern end of the island which had led to some spirited arguments with a Palma ornithologist …

'John, there's something I want to talk about.'

He looked round, surprised by the tone of her voice.

She tapped the letter on her lap. 'This is from an old friend back in England, mainly to say that my godfather, Geoffrey Maitland, who's been ill for a long time, can't last much longer. It's to be hoped the doctors are right because he's suffered long enough. He's ninety-one, so he's had a long innings.'

She looked tiredly old herself, he thought, as he wondered where the conversation was leading.

She drank, then carefully lit a cigar. 'He's a cantankerous old man and has rowed with practically everyone, including his few relations: funnily enough, though, he and I got on very well together and when my husband died he immediately asked if I needed financial help. Perhaps it was a case of Greek appreciating Greek.' She smiled momentarily. 'Or maybe it's because we only saw each other at long intervals. Anyway, cutting a long story short, he said years ago that he was going to leave the bulk of his fortune to me, and his relations — all of whom are far too wealthy for their own good as it is — wouldn't get anything much unless I dropped dead before he did. He's not a man to change his mind without saying he has so that I imagine that's how his estate is still willed. He's very rich because he's cantankerous — always delighted in doing what the experts advised against.'

'That will be great for you.' He was genuinely glad and sounded it.

She played with the letter and for a while was noticeably uncertain about what to say. Then she spoke abruptly. 'I don't need any more money, John. My husband left me a life interest in family money — which goes back to his family as we never had any children — and it's more than enough for me because I've never gone in for jewellery or longed to sail around the world on a luxury cruise.' She chuckled. 'The only thing I really would like to do is buy a Rolls to park alongside and overwhelm the Eastmores'

Daimler. Nearly gives her fatal blood pressure when I remind her it's only a Jaguar and what Jaguars were called before the war … So I've what money I need and on top of that I've a rooted objection to dying and leaving a load of money which the government pinches. I'm going to give Geoffrey's money to you.'

He stared at her, utterly surprised.

She spoke quietly. 'When you came here you were someone who'd been kicked around by life and knocked down. I knew just how you felt because I had a husband who died. But one day you talked farming to me and you changed and came alive. You told me all about your past battles and what the future could be if only you'd the capital. I saw you were a dreamer like your father, but unlike him you were a dreamer who could go out and translate those dreams into reality by sheer hard gutsy work. I saw something almost unknown on this island — a man with enough enthusiasm to have a vision.

'Talk to any of the English out here about being a visionary and they'll think you're talking about LSD, or whatever the latest drug craze is. But I want you to grab that vision with both hands. Which is why I'm going to give you the money and why I've had my solicitors make a new will just in case anything happens to me before Geoffrey's estate is finally settled.'

He said: 'You've just about shattered me.'

She smiled broadly, with happiness, and suddenly her round, vein-laced, rough-complexioned face, set beneath straggly greying hair, held a softness that many people would not have believed possible. 'How much would the dream farm of yours cost?'

'Complete, equipped down to the last harrow, a quarter of a million pounds,' he answered immediately. He'd worked out the figures often enough — playing the game, Suppose I won the pools. 'But that's perfection. Corners can be cut, or machines left out if one's willing to work that much harder. The basic essentials are good land and good cows and if you don't economize on them, you'll make it. Modern specialized buildings are obviously the best, but if you have to make do with something built in the 'twenties …'

'I doubt you'll need to bother about cutting corners, John.'

'You really think there'll be as much as quarter of a million?'

'Unless Geoffrey suddenly made some very bad investments, that and more. Even after the death-duty sharks have had their pounds of flesh.'

'Good God!' he said, and the words were almost a prayer. 'A farm of really good loam, all drained, and cows able to be out a month earlier and a month later than on clay ... His expression changed. 'Elvina, you really mean it?'

'You surely know me well enough now to be certain I do?'

'But it's something that just doesn't happen. People don't give fortunes away.'

'Sometimes they do. If they're old and content with what they've got and if they meet someone they like very much who has a wonderful enthusiasm and a dream which money can make reality. In any case, it's not all altruism.' Her voice roughened slightly as it regained some of its normal astringency, almost as if she were ashamed of her emotions. 'Like all old people, I'm beginning to want to know I'll leave some sort of monument behind when I die to prove my life wasn't meaningless. Your farm will be my monument. When you've bought it, I'll come over one day and stay with you and you can show me the fields, the hedges, the trees, the cowsheds, the cows, and you can tell me all your plans, and I'll see a future in which I'll be a pan even though my body's a heap of ashes.'

'You're a fraud, Great-Aunt Elvina,' he said softly. 'You play a part out here, yet really you're just a visionary and an idealist.'

'Tell that to Mary Eastmore!' she said abruptly.

*

It was night. Through the opened window of his back bedroom, Tatham looked out across the short stretch of matorral at the nearest mountain. In the moonlight, this had lost its hard profiles and was softened and more friendly. He could see the shadows of the few pine-trees which clung to the precipitous sides in odd places, making him wonder why seeds bothered to grow there and what sustenance these trees could possibly draw out of the bleak limestone. A Scops owl called several times, sounding like a pure-toned bell. There was, thrice repeated, a deep mewing note which he tentatively identified as a hoopoe's.

Life could be staggeringly odd, he thought, recognizing this was not an original conclusion. He had suffered the death of his fiancee, had thrown over the farm as he finally recognized the hopeless proposition it was, had come out here simply because his mother had suggested it ... And as a result he was being offered the chance to own a proper farm, something that could never have happened if he'd stayed at home.

He had no doubts that Elvina meant what she'd said. She and he had hit it off together as soon as they'd met. He had enjoyed her unusual ways because he had always disliked conformity, she had found some quality in him — enthusiasm, dedication, call it what one would — that she equally liked. When the money from her godfather came to her, she was going to pass it on.

He continued to stare at the mountain, but he no longer saw it. Instead, his mind visualized fields of rye grass, long and juicy and beginning to head, forage harvesters chopping the grass and blowing it into tipping trailers, trailers emptying their loads into tower silos, sleek Friesians with the stamp of breeding, milk spurting into the glass jars of a herringbone parlour ...

CHAPTER VII

IT WAS the night of Good Friday and the bells of Llueso's church had been ringing intermittently since dawn. In the floodlit monastery on the hill — looking ethereal since it seemed to float in the middle of black sky — the monks prayed with special devotion.

Tatham, wearing a polo-neck sweater because it was quite cold, had been ready to leave Ca'n Manin for the past half hour when there was a knock at the front door. He went through to the hall, expecting to find the caller was Judy, but instead he met a small, rather dumpy man with a Vandyke beard, a large, flat parcel under his left arm, who said: 'Señor Ingham?' He spoke rapidly in Spanish.

'I'm sorry,' said Tatham in English, 'but this isn't Señor Ingham's house. He lives up the road.'

The man shook his head.

Tatham turned and called out: 'Elvina, can you come? There's a chap wants Lawrence Ingham's place but doesn't speak English.'

She entered the hall from the sitting-room. The man half bowed, his eyes filled with open curiosity as he stared at her unkempt appearance. He spoke as he straightened up and she answered briefly. He bowed again, said goodbye, and returned to his car which he had parked on the patio.

'Mallorquins can't find their way around anywhere,' she said. 'Lawrence told him the first drive on the left after the S-bend-so he comes straight down the dirt-track on the right before the S-bend. Tends to prove Columbus was born on this island since he found America when he was looking for India.'

He laughed, as the car drove off. 'It's not peculiar to Mallorca. Father can lose his way on a dead straight road.'

'I've a soft spot for your father, John, but he's the most impractical man I know … It's odd. That man somehow reminds me of him … Anyway, I'm sure I've never seen the man before.' She shook her head. 'I can't have done and he certainly didn't regard me with recognition!' She looked at her watch. 'Judy ought to have picked you up by now. Every once in a while something odd happens and one of these processions starts on time.'

51

'I'm sorry you won't come with us.'

'I've seen this procession often enough. Bring Judy in for a drink afterwards, won't you? She's refreshingly different and not the crook that stepfather of hers is.'

'I thought you'd got on rather well with Lawrence the other evening when we went to his place for drinks?'

'Only because he wasn't trying to sell me anything. Normally he's pleasant enough, but try and do business with him … He's like all the other foreigners out here who are illegally in the property racket. They'd sell you a tumble-down casita as a manor house if you were blind. It makes me furious. I've seen a few nice people come out here, without much money, and I've seen them swindled by people like Lawrence. I've tried to warn them when I've known in time. D'you know what they've said? "But he's English, so we can trust him." And they think I'm just a crabby old woman who's trying to stir up trouble.'

'I wonder …' he began, but at that moment they heard a car draw up to a stop. 'It must be Judy this time,' he said. 'I'll be seeing you.'

He left the house just as Judy climbed out of her white Seat 600. 'I'm always late for everything,' she said, 'but as I'm not as late as I usually am, I'm early.'

'That, no doubt, explains why I've only been waiting for three-quarters of an hour.'

'Didn't Elvina tell you that nothing ever starts on time out here?'

'On the contrary, she said that occasionally a procession did.'

'That's just Elvina being difficult. I'll eat my latest Patou hat if anything happens before an hour's up. Still, get in and let's move — we'll have to park away back from the route because the place will be seething with people now the procession's been declared to be of special interest by the Ministry of Information and Tourism. I do wish they wouldn't do that sort of thing. In next to no time, the procession will be put on for the tourists and not for the people.'

'And isn't it now?'

'No, it definitely isn't, as you'll see for yourself if I can ever persuade you to get into the car.'

He climbed into the passenger seat.

'Do you mind being driven by a woman?' she asked, as she settled behind the wheel.

'That depends on the woman.'

'Then sit back and relax. I've been driving out here for three years and not had a single accident, so I'm brilliant.'

They parked in Llueso in front of one of the many buildings in which cottage industries were carried out during the day, walked through the square and then past the church to Calle Mayor. Here, the crowds were thick.

'Well?' she demanded. 'Is anything happening yet?'

Being so much taller than the average Mallorquin, he could look over the heads of those in front of him. The centre of the road was clear of anyone but two members of the Municipal police. 'No sign of anything.'

'Then you can apologize for all your unnecessary worrying and start pushing: we want to get through to the steps which are a hundred yards along on the right. As this is Spain, use your elbows and tread on toes if people won't move, but apologize profusely every time.'

They reached the foot of the stone steps which led up to the top of Puig Llueso, the small chapel, and the figure of Christ on the Cross.

The procession began soon after their arrival and almost immediately he realized that Judy had been right; this wasn't a pageant merely carried out to entertain the watching crowds. This was a deeply felt religious experience for those who took part in the procession and for those of faith who watched.

The priest came first, followed immediately by the Virgin of Llueso beneath her golden canopy, carried by four men in white. Town dignitaries, ex-servicemen with medals clanging, the choir, Christ on the Cross carried by one man who staggered under the weight, and the town band playing a dirge, followed. Finally, there walked the penitents. Two abreast, dressed in white robes and with white or green hoods in which eyeholes were cut, many barefoot, they descended the stone stairs, hoods bobbing in unison to each step, some leaving behind smears of blood because the soles of their feet had been cut by the rough stone.

The Mallorquins in the watching crowd became silent and only the foreigners talked amongst themselves.

Judy tucked her arm round his. 'It's eerie,' she whispered.

It *was* eerie. For him, the centuries rolled back, the Inquisition existed, sin had meaning, and only painful expiation could save a man from eternal damnation.

*

The Easter weekend was fine, yet on the following Friday the clouds rolled in before a northerly wind and settled on the mountains to blanket their tops, the light dimmed, lightning flashed, and the rain began.

Ingham stared through the window of the study of Ca'n Xema and cursed the rain, now lashing down with tropical intensity. Soon the mountains, already turned black by the wet, would begin to bear waterfalls, the torrentes would swirl into life with debris-laden floodwater, roads would flood and perhaps become impassable, dirt-tracks would turn into quagmires, and houses would begin to leak. When it rained like this the island became sad and bedraggled, the last place on earth where a man would spend a great deal of money to buy a holiday home. And today the Nauperts were coming to look at the house.

Why couldn't the bloody rain have held off for another day? If even the gods had turned against him, what chance had he of escaping his present bad luck? He looked up, incredibly trying to find some sign of a break in the clouds, and saw only dirty greyness from which the rain bucketed down with even greater intensity.

The Mercedes turned into the drive, windscreen-wipers working with frenzied speed. He hurried into the hall and picked up the two umbrellas he had put ready. He opened the seven-foot-high thick wooden front doors, carved on both sides, and rain thrown up from the ground spattered his feet even in the shelter of the porch. He opened the umbrellas and went out to hand them to the Nauperts, becoming fairly wet in the process.

Back in the hall, he laughed lightly and said in German, one of four languages he spoke fluently: 'The weather's decided to get all of the year's rain over and done with in one day. It'll be blazing sunshine tomorrow.' Anything to dispel a little of the gloom.

Naupert, with slow and careful movements, collapsed the umbrella, then looked for a stand. He frowned briefly when he failed to see one. He was a man of medium height, stocky in build, with a square face filled with sharp, harsh lines. His eyes were pale brown and they had a disconcerting habit of suddenly going blank, as if he'd lost interest in whatever was being said and had retreated into his own thoughts. His wife, of the same height, was fashionably slim despite being well into middle age, was dressed with expensive taste, and her hair and skin were in a condition that spoke of constant care.

'Such a shame to get a day like this,' said Ingham. 'I was looking forward to showing you round the garden — I'm very proud of it. A garden does so much for a house: provides the setting, like the gold of a diamond ring.' The laboured simile produced no noticeable reaction. 'But maybe you'll have time to come some other day and see it?'

Naupert said nothing.

'Suppose we start looking round upstairs?' suggested Ingham. He took them round the bedrooms, pointed out the different hand-made tiles in the bathrooms, the different and traditional patterns carved on the doors. They went up into the square tower. From there, he told them gaily, one could normally see the bay so clearly it was as if one could stretch out and dangle one's fingers in it. Right then, replied Naupert briefly, it was as if the bay were being emptied over them. No goddamn soul, thought Ingham.

He led the way downstairs to the sub-basement and the large area which he had equipped as a traditional English pub. 'Every house needs a folly and this is mine.'

Naupert nodded. He agreed, it was indeed a folly. You stupid bastard, thought Ingham, you can change it into a Munich beer garden, can't you, if that's what turns you on, and import a couple of Brünhildes in size forty-five breastplates?

They left the English bar and went upstairs to inspect the maids' quarters, the washroom, the storerooms, the deep-freeze and refrigerator room, and the kitchen. In the kitchen, Frau Naupert spoke for the first time since saying hallo. She pointed to the space between the two cookers (one electric with automatic timing and cleaning, one working on bottled gas for times of power cuts) and said with distaste: 'There is a dead cockroach.'

It wasn't a cockroach, but one of the many varieties of flying insects which abounded on the island: he failed, however, to convince her of that.

He led them into the music room and switched on the hi-fi. In honour of their arrival, he'd put on Beethoven's Fifth. Naupert said he didn't like Beethoven. Ingham switched off the hi-fi and became possessed of the gloomy certainty that his trump card, the fake Renoir, was going to turn out to be just a joker in this no-joker game.

In the sitting-room, he stood in the centre, behind the circular settee, and pointed out that the fireplace with its beautiful marble surround was fully functional even though the central heating was more than adequate: some people liked the cheerfulness of crackling flames, quite apart from the heat. He noticed that Naupert was staring at the wall where hung the three paintings and suddenly felt a shade more cheerful: at least the fish's attention had been attracted by the dangling bait.

'Will you come and have a look at the windows just to see the point I've mentioned: that I've made the builders use only seasoned wood of first class quality. In most houses out here, they reckon a window fits provided there isn't a gap bigger than a centimetre. I think these windows fit as well as any back home.'

Frau Naupert walked across the room with him, but Naupert merely stepped several paces closer to the Renoir. Softly, softly, catchee monkee, thought Ingham. This isn't fly-fishing, this is deep-sea fishing. He spoke to Frau Naupert. 'From here, of course, you've virtually the same view as from the tower. And I've been around the world a bit, but I honestly don't think I've seen anything to beat it. There are places with starker views on a larger and grander scale, but they all seem to get a bit too awesome. Here, everything is in just the right proportions to be comfortable and friendly. Come here after months of hard work and intense pressure and one can feel the tiredness sloughing off. It's worth a fortune just to enjoy that.'

'The view is useless when it's raining and you cannot see it,' she said.

Lady, he thought, it's people like you who give capitalism a bad name. He laughed. 'On a day like this — which happens maybe once in five years — all one really wants to do is remain in bed.' With someone a hell of a lot less sharp than you, he thought.

She became chatty. 'It is a very expensive house to run.'

'I wouldn't agree, especially when you consider what a place like this would cost you in Germany.'

'I would not have a place like this in Germany.'

Naupert called out loudly. 'How much are you asking?'

'As it is, with all its present furnishings and equipment, twenty million.'

'Twenty million?' repeated Naupert, as if he'd been stung.

'It may sound a lot, but this house is unique, both in itself and its situation. There's not another place on the island to equal it.'

'Twenty million pesetas is very nearly nine hundred thousand marks.'

Ingham nodded.

'It is a —' Naupert seemed to be about to say one thing, then changed his mind — 'a very great deal of money. You are asking that much with all the furnishings as presently exist?'

'Yes. There are, of course, some things which are personal to me or my stepdaughter.'

'What, for instance, would you call personal in this room?'

Ingham smiled. 'Only the bottles in the bar! Everything else, carpets, tapestries, curtains, chairs, tables, knick-knacks, paintings … Though I doubt you'd want them around.' Should he get more specific, he wondered? In for a penny, in for a pound. 'In particular, that Renoir.'

'The — er — Renoir?' said Naupert, suddenly slightly uncertain.

'That's what the one in the centre is supposed to be. Apparently it's got a name, but I can never remember it.'

'*La Premiere Sortie*,' murmured Naupert, then his eyes flicked a look at Ingham and his expression suggested he was annoyed at himself for having spoken.

'That's it! The friend I showed it to told me the name, but for some peculiar reason I always forget it. Funny, isn't it, how there seem to be certain simple things which one can never remember?'

Naupert took a crocodile-skin cigar case from his inside coat pocket, was about to take one when he checked himself and offered a cigar to Ingham, who refused, chose one for himself and took painstaking care in clipping the end and lighting the cigar. 'You say you showed the painting to a friend? Had you some particular reason?'

'I had, but it's one of those reasons which are somewhat embarrassing to bring out in the cold light of day!' He lit a cigarette. 'It may be a bit early, but it's such a terrible day a drink seems the only antidote. Can I persuade you to have one?'

Frau Naupert said: 'Thank you, but I …' Her husband interrupted her. 'Thank you, that will be an excellent idea. I would like a scotch and my wife always prefers a sweet vermouth with a dash of soda and a slice of lemon.'

Ingham suggested they sat and he went through to the small bar and poured out the drinks, which he handed round on a tray. He sat down in one of the chairs and raised his glass. 'Here's to everybody.' Had the bait been tweaked expertly enough?

Ash slid off Naupert's cigar and trickled down the front of his beautifully tailored green light-weight jacket. He took off his unrimmed glasses and polished the lenses with a handkerchief.

Ingham began to chat about a holiday he had had in Cochem.

'A nice little town,' said Naupert, dismissing the subject. He drew on the cigarette, then said: 'You mentioned that you had a particular reason for showing the painting. I'm sure it's an interesting reason?'

'Well, I don't mind publicly putting on a fool's cap for a little! After all, I'm not the first person to have had big ideas … I found the painting when I was down in Perpignan a few years back. I was rooting around in an old junk shop — you know, the kind of place there used to be in most countries before antiques became such big news: everything from a rusty piece of armour to a broken-down zither. There were a load of paintings ranged against a wall and I looked through them and saw that one. I've always liked the Impressionists and this one seemed a very attractively-done copy of something that was quite familiar. I remember having a stab at naming the painter and came up with Cezanne, which shows how much I know! Anyway, I had a good old bargain and ended up by buying the painting for the equivalent of a couple of pounds.

'When I got home and had another look at it, I suddenly began to get the wild idea that I might have discovered an original. There was something, maybe the authority of the work, that seemed so much above the ordinary copy. I guess we all day-dream about finding an old master or a Ming vase. I took the painting along to a friend who's an art teacher at a polytechnic and asked him what he thought of it. He identified it immediately as Renoir and showed me a reproduction of the original in one of his art books … That's when we found in this one that the girl's dress is slightly different, especially the very flowing hat and the cuffs, and that the man on the left isn't looking the girl's way — which apparently has always caused a bit of a mystery. I said why should there be these slight differences unless this was an earlier study? He looked at me and roared with laughter. Asked me whether I really thought it could be a genuine Renoir? I denied that, of course. He didn't believe me and told me to look at the quality of the brush-work and said that if he couldn't do better than that he'd give up art teaching. I tried to get him to suggest a reason for the differences between the copy and the original, but he wasn't interested. So I took my copy away and kept it out of sight until I was furnishing this room. I know it's a crude copy, but it looks gay … Sentiments which must offend you?'

Naupert replaced his glasses. 'It would be interesting to know why the copyist changed certain features.' He stood up and crossed to the painting and studied it closely, even turning it round to examine the back. He shrugged his shoulders. 'No doubt the whim of a man who reckoned he knew so much better than the master.' He returned to his chair.

'How about another drink?' offered Ingham.

'I think not, thank you. I seldom have more than one. Herr Ingham, you understand that I should not consider buying any property without having it completely surveyed and the title-deeds examined by my own experts?'

'Of course.'

'And if I were at all interested in buying this house, the price would have to be a matter of negotiation?'

The bait had been snapped, thought Ingham: hook him tight. 'No, I'm sorry, I never negotiate a price. I add a reasonable profit on to site and building costs and that has to be that.'

Naupert fiddled with his cigar. He began to look towards the wall on which hung the Renoir, but stopped himself. 'That is a point which could be discussed at some later date, should there be reason to do so. I would like two friends of mine to come and survey this house. That will be in order?'

'They can check anything they want, for as long as they want.' One of them would be a surveyor, thought Ingham, but the other would be an art expert. His sole job would be surreptitiously to examine the Renoir to authenticate it, or dismiss it, in so far as this could be done by visual examination only. If Antonio Galan's boast proved to be justified — that the fake was so good it would defy all but a couple of experts in the world, and maybe even them — then Naupert could be reeled in, gaffed, and landed. No one was greedier than a rich man.

CHAPTER VIII

MARIE MAYANS, small, petite, light-brown hair which was unusual for a Mallorquin, with a figure which rigid dieting kept slim, said, with much emphasis: 'No.' She put a new price tab on a mock-antique sword.

'You're being very stupid,' said her husband loudly.

'Am I?' She came out from behind the counter. 'And have you any other kind compliments for me?'

He was too annoyed to heed her tone of voice. 'I keep telling you, this foreigner will pay two million for the field.'

'Maybe. But he will have to come and tell me that, to my face.'

'Tell you? Why should he tell you? I'm the man in the house.'

'Oh yes, you're the man!' She put her hands on her hips. 'You're the man who spends all his time in the Llueso Club drinking cognac and comes back all mutton-headed as though it were his Saint's Day. I'm just the woman of the house. I just open the shop and work from dawn to midnight in order to buy food which I cook for you and you never eat because you're too filled with cognac fumes. We all know who the man is in this house. Isn't that right, Dolores?' She turned and called across to the teenage girl who worked as an assistant in the shop for the spring and summer season.

Dolores giggled.

'Are you saying I don't work myself sick?' he demanded furiously.

'Work yourself sick? That's a wonderful idea. You're sick most of the time, right enough, but it's from cognac, not work.'

'I go into Palma and buy at the flea market, I go round the towns and buy cast-off furniture, I make things, I talk to representatives …'

'And offer them a cognac so that you can start swilling. Your guts must be more pickled than the cask the cognac comes in.'

Dolores giggled again.

He ran his hand through his short, crinkly black hair. 'On the Peninsula,' he said furiously, 'you would be nobody.

The fields, the fincas, and the shop would be mine. If you dared speak like that, I'd put a whip across your back.'

'But I'm not a Spaniard, I'm a Mallorquin, this is not the Peninsula, it is Mallorca, and by our law the fields, the fincas, and the shop are mine, even though I've suffered the terrible misfortune of being married to you. And you try to put a whip across my back and I'll land a pair of scissors in that fat, cognac-pickled belly of yours.'

He stalked over to the door of the shop. A party of three tourists, English to judge by the gauche clothes the woman was wearing, stopped outside and poked around in one of the trays of olive wood knick-knacks. They left and returned to the pavement. He turned back and shouted at his wife: 'Two million pesetas for a field worth a quarter of a million.'

No Mallorquin, not even an indignant wife, could resist the lure of money. 'And where did you meet this rich foreigner?' she asked sarcastically. 'In one of the back bars and after the fifth cognac so that his wits were as befuddled as yours?'

'He's Dutch and he has a big car and he wants to build a very big house. He likes the land because it's clear of the shadow of the mountain until very late at night.'

'You've taken him along to see it, have you?'

'And why shouldn't I?'

'No doubt you told him it was your land and you'd sell it to him?'

'I just fixed the price.'

'Two million? In cash?'

'In cash.'

'It's not land that's good for anything else,' she said slowly.

'With two million you could build a house to make Carmen spit with fury.'

Marie walked slowly back to the counter and she tapped her fingers on the studs of the hand-operated adding machine. Carmen was her sister-in-law. She'd be so jealous, she'd be miserable for weeks and weeks. 'Bring the Dutchman along so that I can talk to him.'

'There's no need. I've discussed the matter fully. He'll pay two million, in cash, for the field.'

'But he'll pay me the two million, not you.'

'I have arranged —' he began.

'And from now on I will arrange. D'you think I'd dare let you manage anything, after the mess you made of Ca'n Manin? If I let you manage this affair, you'd sell the field for a hundred thousand.'

Dolores giggled.

He lost his temper and called his wife a lot of names he was subsequently to regret. Some of his resentment stemmed from the fact that the Dutchman had agreed to pay two and a half million.

*

'You really do have such a lovely house here, Mary,' said Mrs Cabbott. 'It's quite the most lovely house I know. But then you have such taste.' She was large and bulging, blue-rinsed her hair, and wore a double rope of pearls.

Lady Eastmore thought it was odd she could exhibit such bad taste as to praise excessively. She summoned a maid with the portable bell push and ordered two more drinks.

They sat by the pool, now free of all rose petals, in the hot sunshine which had succeeded the torrential rain. A light breeze from the north came over the mountain to rustle the fronds of the palm trees, but the pool was protected by the glass and brick wall which backed the whole of the complex. Freed of wind, the day was hot and Mrs Cabbott was noticeably sweating.

'I met the new people who've moved into Ca'na Amoza,' said Mrs Cabbott. 'Letty asked me to coffee and never told me they'd be there: so unthoughtful of her not to warn me. Of course, she's half American and they are so impulsive.' The maid brought them two fresh drinks and took away the empty glasses.

Lady Eastmore ate the queen olive which had been in her Martini. 'What were these new people like?'

'Oh dear, it was so very difficult. We knew absolutely no one in common so there was nothing to talk about: no mental touching point, if you know what I mean?' She paused. 'The man writes some sort of books and the woman was dressed badly. So depressing to meet those kind of people.'

Lady Eastmore lit a cigarette as they heard a car draw up in front of the house. Shortly afterwards, Brigadier Gabbott and Lord Eastmore came round the side of the house.

'Freddie beat me two and one,' said Lord Eastmore. 'I really must order a new putter from home.'

'You'll need a whole new set of clubs, Charles, before you've any chance of beating me,' replied Cabbott breezily. He was a tall, thin, cadaverous-looking man with the cheerful ignorance of a retired officer from one of the better regiments.

'What'll you have, Freddie?' asked Lord Eastmore.

'I could really murder a pint. Haven't any Red Barrel, have you, by some miracle?'

'Of course we have,' said Lady Eastmore in gentle reproof. 'We have it specially imported.'

'My God! My guts are aching at the thought already.'

'I'll have a long G and T,' said Lord Eastmore.

Lady Eastmore rang the buzzer, and when the maid hurried up, she gave the order.

'Heard about Guy?' demanded Cabbott, as he relaxed in a cane chair and stretched out his long, thin legs. 'You know he's as short-sighted as an angry rhino? The silly bastard didn't wear his specs when he was doing his swimming pool and he picked up a carboy of gin instead of the usual chlorine. He poured it all in. Everyone who went in swimming came out plastered, what!'

Lord Eastmore smiled indulgently, Lady Eastmore was frostily not amused, and Mrs Cabbott kicked her husband's ankle.

'Steady on, old girl,' said Cabbott. 'Charles, d'you hear about old Morley? That Bank of England imshi turned up at his house and started asking very nasty questions. Of course, old Morley said he didn't know anything, but. this bloody imshi seemed to know the lot: even told him how much capital he'd shifted out illegally in the past year.'

'Awkward,' said Lord Eastmore.

'You ought to hear old Morley's language. Make my old RSM turn green with envy. Of course, he's facing God knows what fines. The bloody imshi even knew about the bank account in Switzerland.'

'Good God! But the Swiss bank surely couldn't have disclosed the account?'

'Not them. No, it's some bloody little gobbins-tiki here who's been talking.'

'Gobbins-tiki? Been talking? What do you mean?' demanded Lady Eastmore.

'These imshis are like the slat-wallahs in the income-tax at home who learn all about tax evasions from anonymous tip-offs. You know how it goes, Mary. Someone living here is jealous so he or she writes an anonymous letter to say old Morley keeps boasting about how he putt-putts all his money out of England.'

'Don't be so ridiculous. No one could be so undignified as to do such a thing.'

'You'd be surprised. As I've always said, you can't beat human nature for tricks. Someone suggested the gobbins-tiki was Elvina — she could be crazy enough, couldn't she, Charles?'

'What's that?' asked Lord Eastmore.

Cabbott roared with laughter. 'Got you fair and square in the oogles, has it? Wondering if anyone is denouncing you for all the money you've … Jesus!' he exclaimed as he bent down to rub his ankle where his wife had kicked it even harder than before.

'You'd never ever do such a thing, Mary,' said Mrs Cabbott, with passionate loyalty. 'It's absolutely unthinkable. Freddie, how can you be so stupid? Someone in Charles and Mary's position would never, ever break the law.'

The Queen, like Caesar's wife, was beyond suspicion: else she could not be the queen. They all knew that.

*

The rain returned, not the thundery, torrential downpour of several days ago but a steady drizzle that would not have been out of place in Manchester. Tatham drove to the post-office in Llueso and collected the mail, bought a two-litre flagon of red wine and a barra for the picnic and wondered why, in any country, the finest rain-maker was a proposed picnic? Maybe that was what came of arranging a day out with Judy. Yet he couldn't really believe that, even though he'd just forwarded the proposition.

He drove slowly back along the main road — the roads were dressed for hot sun, not rain, and became treacherous when wet: every Mallorquin knew that, none heeded the fact — passing a car that had spun off the road into the scrubland to the side, turned on to the Creyola road and soon after that into the narrow lane which led to the dirt-track and Ca'n Manin. Spring was well under way. Fig trees were showing green tips, pomegranate and walnut trees were sprouting, vines were in full bud, tomatoes were planted out, some under 'greenhouses' made from homegrown bamboos and plastic sheeting, the first late orange blossom was showing while the trees still bore ripe fruit which, strangely, so often seemed not to be picked, dates which would never ripen were just breaking out of straw-coloured pods … The same kind of reawakening, though earlier, as in England.

He parked the Fiat under the balcony of Ca'n Manin and went inside the house. Elvina was tidying the sitting-room: for one so untidy in her person, she was strangely fussy about the condition of the house. 'Two letters for you,' he said, 'and one looks suspiciously like the inland revenue.'

She straightened up. 'You know what you can do with that!'

He handed her the two letters.

'Would you like some coffee before you go, John?'

'That's a great idea.'

'Would you make it, then, and some for me — I haven't had breakfast yet. Going native, it's called! By the way, I've put all your food on the table.'

He went into the kitchen and prepared the Espresso coffee pot and put it on the stove, then packed into the freezy-bag cheese, butter, ham, mustard, tomatoes, corkscrew, and glasses.

When he returned to the sitting-room, Elvina said: 'Madge has written again. George is very near the end and she'll send a cable when he dies so that I can return in time for the funeral. You won't mind being on your own, will you? You can look after yourself, unlike your father who has never learned how a can-opener works.' She put the letter down. 'I wonder why it sometimes has to take so long to die?'

He imagined a very old man, stubborn face leathered with age, lying in a bed and taking a long, long time to die.

The coffee machine hissed. He asked her if she wanted anything to eat and she said a couple of slices of bread and butter with marmalade. In the kitchen, he poured out two cupfuls of coffee, added sugar and milk, cut the bread and butter, found the pot of marmalade, and carried the tray back into the sitting-room.

'Any idea where you're going today?' asked Elvina.

'None at all. I said I'd leave it entirely up to Judy. Maybe with this rain she'll prefer to cancel.'

'I doubt it. She's not the kind of girl to worry about a little wet. In any case, it's fun seeing the island in the rain because it all looks so different. I said that to someone not so long ago and she looked at me as if I was quite insane. Probably didn't know you could go out when it rained.' She stirred her coffee. 'When you've got the farm running smoothly and can leave it for a time, come and see me out here, John.'

'As often as possible. But you promised to come over to England and see the farm for yourself.'

'Of course I shall, once. But not more than once because I get bronchitis so easily these days if the weather's anything like it usually is over there.

But I want to see you much more than once before my time's up.' She drank some coffee. 'Tell me, which part of the country would you like to go to? Shropshire or Cheshire, which I've always been told are the dairy counties? Or farther south? How about Devonshire, when you could send a regular supply of clotted cream to me? When I was young, that was the greatest treat life had to offer.'

She had not been exaggerating, he thought, when she had told him what the farm would mean to her.

*

It was just before ten o'clock that night when Tatham drove the Fiat on to the loose-surfaced drive of Ca'n Xema and stopped before the front door. He switched off the headlights, but left the engine running.

'I've enjoyed the day, John, and most especially dinner,' said Judy. 'It's been such fun. But you're surely going to come in and have a nightcap?'

'I don't think so, thanks a lot. I'm feeling quite tired.'

'You ought to have let me do some of the driving — even if in your heart of hearts you don't really trust me.' She laughed as she put her hand lightly on his right arm. 'Don't leave it too long before you come and see me again. After all, you're almost the only male under sixty this side of Palma: the only guaranteed male, that is. Good night.' She climbed out too quickly for him to try to help her, waved once, crossed to the door and let herself in.

He switched on the headlights, backed, turned, and drove out. Judy was a strangely difficult person to pinpoint, he thought. Sometimes she was hard and cynical, sometimes much softer in outlook and easily pleased. Always, he sensed a mental strain which, for no particular reason other than a brief and unfinished conversation, he believed had something to do with Lawrence Ingham. 'He's usually great fun,' she'd said, 'but ...' Then she'd stopped and changed the conversation.

He went round the S-turn, down the very short straight, and left on to the dirt-track. The headlights picked out fig-trees and the distorted prickly pear cacti, the fruit of both now seldom picked as a direct result of the rising standard of living. He followed round by the wall of the next property — behind this was a pig pen and an electric pump used for irrigation purposes — and up to the estanque. When lie turned right, the headlights picked out the house and patio and he saw a bundle lying by a pillar of the balcony, near one of the garden chairs. It wasn't until he was about to turn into the garage that he realized the bundle was a body.

CHAPTER IX

ELVINA, dressed in blue woollen frock, tights, muddy walking shoes, lay half curled up in an untidy huddle and the top of her head was in a state that made him feel sick, even though he was used to bloody wounds in animals. Underneath her head was a length of bamboo on to which she'd fallen and by her side was a section of the wooden rails of the balcony. He stepped back and looked up. In the lights of the car, he could see where the wooden rails had broken and where a further section hung loose. A small trickle of water dribbled intermittently down from the balcony and this had evidently diluted and washed away the blood, for little remained.

He stared at the body as he tried to clear his mind sufficiently to decide what to do. Get hold of a doctor? She was beyond any doctor's help although obviously a doctor must be called. But, knowing no doctor, wasn't his obvious move to go into Llueso and inform the police so that they could organize everything?

What a way to die! Then he revised his thoughts. She would have known only a brief second of panic as she leaned against the wooden railing and felt it give, to fall head first below. Most people were not so lucky.

He felt he needed something to steady his nerves and quell a rising nausea and in any case an extra five minutes could mean nothing to her. He went into the house and switched on the lights, returned to the car and switched off the headlights, then went through to the larder and poured himself out a very large brandy and swallowed it quickly. He lit a cigarette and gratefully dragged the smoke down into his lungs.

Which police did he go to? The Municipal police or the Guardia Civil? He didn't really know what was the difference between them, but he did know where were the offices of the Municipal police. Hopefully, he'd find someone there who could understand English.

Elvina had told him only a few days ago that the wooden rails of the balcony were in a very poor state. 'Like all the other wood in the house,' she'd said, 'ravaged by woodworm and rotting from neglect. I first mentioned them to Jose a couple of years back. He promised to get the carpenter right away. Maybe in two years' time the man will actually turn up. Maybe.' The carpenter had left his visit too late.

He would have liked a second brandy, but decided against it. He must have a clear head.

He left the kitchen and went into the sitting-room, finished his cigarette, stubbed it out, and immediately lit another. It was no good telephoning the police since he didn't speak Spanish: much better to go in person and ... It suddenly occurred to him that it seemed probable no telegram had arrived to announce the death of Geoffrey Maitland.

Maitland had left Elvina the bulk of his fortune provided only that she did not predecease him. As there had been quite a disparity in their ages, such a possibility must have seemed remote. Yet, against the odds, this had probably happened. (A check to see whether she had packed, a search of her handbag for the telegram, these would show if the news had come through.) So the fortune wouldn't be coming through her to him. There would be no hundred and fifty acres of lush grass, supporting a hundred and fifty sleek-hided cows ...

A dream had been shattered for all time when she fell from the balcony. He remembered her pleasure at being able to give him pleasure and how she'd told him, speaking lightly and ironically yet not quite able to conceal the fact that she meant what she was saying, that the farm would be her memorial, something to give her life a lasting meaning. With his dream had gone her memorial. He must either return to a rented farm that wouldn't be big enough or good enough to be properly profitable or work for someone else, and her only memorial would be a tombstone on this island which would be read by no one.

Perhaps, by some miracle, Geoffrey Maitland had died first? But a telegram surely wouldn't take long to arrive and Madge had promised to send word as soon as he died. The house had been in darkness so that Elvina must have fallen after Catalina had left, but before dark.

He was a man who dreamed, yet who could set aside his dreams when there was no chance of their becoming reality. For a few days a farm had been his and in his mind he'd stocked and cultivated it, but now it no longer existed. He was back to the position in which he'd been ...

The idea flashed through his mind and his initial reaction was to dismiss it as a sick fantasy. But the idea remained with him. Suppose Elvina's death was not immediately disclosed? Geoffrey Maitland must die very soon. Provided only that she appeared to have outlived him, the money would come to her and she had said that she'd made certain her estate was willed through so that the farm could be his whatever happened. Maitland's relatives would lose their inheritance, but then they were all apparently more than wealthy enough already. So what would the loss mean to them other than forgoing the greedy pleasure the rich man gained when his riches increased?

What about the indignity Elvina's body might have to suffer? He seemed to hear her harsh laughter. 'Indignity? Gobbledegook! A dead body is a hunk fit for nothing but providing spare parts or turning into fertilizer. If my body can be of use, use it. Get that farm and remember me when you're ploughing the twenty-acre field.'

But how did one conceal a death, even for twenty-four hours? Because he had dealt with large animals, he knew that the irreversible signs of death came very quickly and could not be missed. If her body was twenty-four hours dead, no doctor could be deceived into believing death had only just taken place. And was it realistic to think in terms of twenty-four hours? Old people often took longer to die than anyone would have believed possible. It might be days and days before Maitland died. And if the weather turned hot ...

There'd been a cow which had aborted at the beginning of the August Bank Holiday weekend when the nearby diagnostic veterinary laboratories had been closed, but he'd needed the foetus tested for contagious abortion. He'd wrapped up the foetus in plastic and put it in an old and no longer used refrigerated milk cooler. The foetus had kept perfectly ... There was a very large deep-freeze out in the wash-shed ...

He went through to the larder and poured himself out the second brandy he had denied himself earlier. So few people came to see Elvina that she could be missing for days without comment, except from Catalina who worked five afternoons a week. But Elvina's absence each afternoon could easily be explained away — picnics. Since he'd arrived Elvina had been out of the house many of the afternoons, driving him around the island. At such times, the only contact Catalina had had with Elvina had been the five hundred pesetas left in an envelope for her each Friday.

Legally, he must surely be committing a crime if he did not report the death immediately, but tried to conceal it? Spanish law could not be very different on that point from English law. But what had the law ever done for him? Killed Jennifer. The law had demanded she testify in court, had promised she'd be guarded from any harm, and had seen her murdered. So to hell with what the law demanded from the honest citizen.

He went from the kitchen into the back garden — a natural rock garden. The washroom was on the right, set out at right angles to the end of the kitchen. In it was an old-fashioned double-tiled sink, a modern washing-machine, and a large deep-freeze with one-piece lid. He lifted the lid — it was lockable, but unlocked — and found the cabinet was about half full of food. That would have to be thrown away, something easily done because there were a hundred and one near-perfect hiding-places out in the scrubland at the back, especially in the area littered with huge boulders up to two metres high.

He bent down and checked the deep-freeze control, set behind a grill on hinges. He turned the control to its coldest setting. The compressor immediately started working. And it was this humming sound, more than his own thoughts, which convinced him he was going to do the bizarre and macabre thing his mind had visualized.

He emptied the cabinet, stacking the food on the concrete floor. What to wrap the body in? There were no large sheets of plastic available, so it would have to be some sort of blanket. This would have the advantage of absorbing any blood before the body became frozen.

He went up to the solar and found the french windows leading out on to the balcony were open and swinging gently to the wind. A little rain had blown in and dampened the concrete floor and one edge of the nearer Ispahan carpet. He remembered, even as he stepped forward, how each day she'd cleaned the carpets by hand. 'Never use a vacuum cleaner on a decent carpet,' she'd once told him, as if this were a really heinous offence. He was about to shut the windows when he remembered the broken rails and he switched on the outside light and stepped out.

Because the concrete floor of the balcony was uneven, water had gathered in a large pool that stretched right across and was too wide for him to step over, yet which wasn't deep. He crossed to the section of broken railing. The design had been quite elaborate, with carved balusters, but typically the balusters at their bases had been too thin so that the wood had had only to rot to a little depth to become unsafe and the way they had been set in the concrete had ensured rain water collected around their bases. One baluster had crashed below, one was leaning over, one section of rails was below and two sections were hanging down but were still just attached. They could, he estimated, all be patched up sufficiently well that nothing would be obvious from down below. He noticed that the exact point at which she'd fallen was marked by a trail in the light dusting of sodden dirt where one of her toe-caps had briefly dragged.

He returned, tried not to step on any of the carpets because his shoes were now very wet and dirty, but couldn't avoid doing so, shut the french windows, switched off the light, and went down to the hall.

In the front downstairs bedroom was a double bed and on this was a multi-coloured cover in rough woven wool that matched the covers on all the other beds and of which he knew there were two spares. He pulled it off the bed and carried it out on to the patio. He laid it out by the side of Elvina's body and then rolled her on to it. He tried to fold her up, but had considerable difficulty, especially with her arms and trunk which had stiffened. Eventually, he succeeded.

The bundle was awkward and caused him considerable difficulty, even though she had been a thin, small woman and he was strong with muscles used to heavy loads. He carried the bundle through the house to the washroom, managed to lift the lid of the deep-freeze with the tips of the fingers of his right hand, and lowered it down. It just fitted. He shut the lid, locked it, and put the key in his pocket. He was sweating more heavily than the exercise warranted and he mopped his face and neck with a handkerchief.

Against the far wall of the washroom was a plastic bucket and broom. He filled the bucket with water and went out to the patio and scrubbed down the pillar and concrete ground, after removing the five-foot-long bamboo, until all traces of blood were gone. He swilled everything down with more water, drawn from the well.

After returning the bucket and broom to the washroom, he poured himself out a third brandy and lit a cigarette. When he'd finished both drink and cigarette, he thought, he must remove and burn the bamboo and make a sufficiently good repair to the rails of the balcony to conceal until the morning, when a much better repair could be carried out, what had happened.

CHAPTER X

THURSDAY'S weather was once more hot and sunny and when Tatham awoke, after a surprisingly good sleep, the sunshine was streaming round the edges of the curtain of the east-facing window. He got out of bed and pulled back the curtain. Beyond the roof of the washroom, made from the same variegated brown and fawn tiles as the roof of the house, was the scrubland in which he had dumped the food the previous night: under the roof was the deep-freeze and in it was Elvina's body. It was truly almost incredible.

He went into the upstairs bathroom and began to run a bath. After a long while the water heated up — the delay was to be expected since the bare hot pipes ran part of their course outside the house — but almost at once it turned cold again, which probably meant that the gas cylinder had run out. He went downstairs and into the back garden and changed the gas cylinder of the water-heater. When he tried to re-light the pilot light, it wouldn't work. He lifted the coupling off the gas cylinder, replaced it, tried the pilot light again and this time it worked. So many things on the island were like that: working or not working arbitrarily. But the deception of Elvina's death had to work.

He had a bath, only just warm enough despite the new gas, dressed, and went downstairs. Over breakfast, he mentally weighed up whether it would be better for him to be in or out, in either case ostensibly with Elvina, for the day: he decided to be out. His mind moved on. Under what conditions should the body finally be found? That must surely depend on how long it would take to unfreeze? If any part of the body remained frozen when it was found, the deception would be over.

He washed up his supper and breakfast china and cutlery — Elvina disliked either to be left lying around — dried them, and put them away in the larder. What next? He suddenly remembered that, strangely in one so tidy about the house, Elvina never bothered to make her bed during the week but left that to Catalina to do in the afternoon. He went up to her bedroom, pulled back the cover, the two blankets, and a sheet, lay on the bottom sheet to crumple it, looked for the pair of pyjamas she had been wearing and found these under the single pillow and left them lying across the bed. What about dirty clothes? She wore old and shapeless frocks, but he felt certain these and her underclothes were always clean so they would be frequently changed. Mostly, she put them in the washing-machine herself. He would do the same and hang the wet clothes out on the line that was strung across the back garden. Food. He must buy enough for the two of them. Bread, meat, butter, milk, etc., could be stored in larder or refrigerator and be used up at a regular rate. Always remembering Elvina had been a surprisingly good trencherwoman. He must buy wine at the usual shop because she never ate a meal without a considerable quantity of wine ... The complications suddenly became endless whereas the previous night the only real problems had seemed to be to get the body into the deep-freeze and repair the balcony rails. To continue. Suppose mail arrived and by its nature had to be answered virtually by return? Would it be better to invent an illness? But an illness severe enough to keep a person out of sight and unable to write a letter must surely be severe enough to call in the doctor? Money. She drew money at irregular intervals from her bank. If the deception had to be kept going for many days, the failure to draw money might attract attention. Could he sign a cheque in her name? A ridiculous suggestion. Then perhaps it should after all be an illness that prevented her going to the bank? But there would be one or two people who, hearing she was ill, would want to know how she was. Other people would want to be seen to be doing the right thing ...

He suddenly needed to check that the deep-freeze lid was locked and he hurried out into the washroom to do this, even though he could clearly remember locking it the previous night. The motor was working, as was to be expected. Until the body was reduced to just below zero, it would work continuously.

Back in the kitchen, he organized a picnic for two. Freezy-bag, with the two cold packs taken from the frozen compartment of the refrigerator, butter, the rest of the sliced ham from the previous day, cheese, tomatoes, mustard, jam — she had the North-Country habit of eating jam with cheese — two knives, two glasses, jar of red wine, bottle of white Cinzano for her, red Cinzano for him, two paper napkins because she hated having greasy fingers ...

He carried the freezy-bag out to the Fiat and put it in the back. Then, even whilst he knew this was ridiculous, he suddenly wondered if the deep-freeze lid was locked. He felt the key in his trousers pocket, but still went back to the washroom to check. Was there a second key? Catalina might know where it was kept. He searched the washroom, but found no key hidden on any ledge.

Elvina's handbag was in the sitting-room and he only noticed it by chance. Yet she would never have gone out for the day without it. He picked it up. For some reason, it reminded him that the cover of the downstairs front bed had not been replaced. He suddenly felt panicky, as if disaster were already sitting on his shoulders. So he stood still, lit a cigarette, and smoked. It was an old trick of his. When things on the farm had gone wrong — the vacuum on the milking plant was too low, but nothing would apparently rectify it-he'd forced himself to take a break, no matter what the pressures, to smoke, and to think out the problem. A moment's calm thought was usually worth an hour's frenzied rushing about. As he smoked, he decided the problems weren't as bad as he'd begun to imagine. Elvina was extremely tidy so the house was never in a mess, but beyond that she was so unpredictable that any departure from normal would raise little curiosity. Acts of omission would surely be put down to her 'peculiarity'.

He found a spare bedcover and put it in the downstairs front bedroom. He left the house, locked the front door, and hung the key on the back of one of the outer wooden doors for Catalina. He climbed into the car, started it, backed out, and drove down the dirt-track. How long would Geoffrey Maitland live, he wondered, as the car bounced into and out of potholes.

*

He returned to Ca'n Manin at six-thirty.

The house bore all the usual signs of Catalina's having been there during the afternoon. Chairs were moved back into the positions in which she reckoned they should be, as opposed to those where Elvina wanted them, fresh flowers — picked from the garden despite repeated requests to leave them growing — were on the wrought-iron and marble table in the sitting-room, all the tiled floors still showed odd pockets of damp from being washed down.

He put the freezy-bag and the jar of wine on the kitchen floor and hurried out to the wash-room. The lid of the deep-freeze was locked and the motor was still working. Was the engine, he wondered, in one of its regular cycles or had it not yet stopped because the temperature was still not low enough? One was usually directed not to put in more than fifteen pounds of produce to be frozen at any one time … Suppose it did break down? Where did one get hold of the service engineer? How to prevent the engineer from lifting the lid to test the temperature …? To hell with all that. There had to be an end to the contingencies against which he planned.

Back in the kitchen, he poured some of the red wine down the sink. Elvina would have had at least three more glassfuls than had been taken out. Should Catalina for some reason see the jar tomorrow, the right amount must have apparently been drunk.

He was about to flush the sink with water when he heard a car approach and then the slam of a door. The next moment, there was a call: 'Anyone at home?' He recognized Judy's voice.

He went through to the hall. She stood just inside, one hand on the front door. She was dressed in grey slacks and woollen sweater and her hair was in a tangle as if blown about by the wind: the only apparent make-up she wore was lipstick.

'Hallo, John. I was beginning to think no one was in.'

'I was through in the kitchen. We've just been on a picnic and I was clearing up.'

'I've called in to talk about cabbages and kings. D'you mind?'

'How d'you mean?' he asked sharply.

She looked at him, then away, and a sulky expression formed round her mouth. 'You obviously don't remember your Carroll. But you're busy, so I'll push on.' She moved to leave.

'Hang on,' he said, trying to sound welcoming.

She stepped into the doorway. 'There's no need to put yourself out. If you'd rather be on your own, for God's sake say so.'

'All this because I didn't remember my Lewis Carroll? What gives, that you take umbrage quicker than a bloke can breathe?'

'I have the unfortunate faculty of knowing when I'm not wanted.'

'Anyone as snappy as you is surely never not wanted?'

She hesitated, then finally smiled. 'You reckon?'

He grinned back at her. 'Feel in a right bitchy mood and want to bitch? Come in and do so to your heart's content, but over a drink.'

She studied his face. 'You're inviting me in for a drink?'

'Yes. Would you like it in writing?'

She finally stepped inside and shut the door.

'Was something the matter?' she asked. 'I mean when I first saw you? You looked … almost hostile?'

'Indigestion,' he replied. 'And if we're trading impressions, you look slightly less than your usual self.'

'I'm not exactly feeling like jumping over the moon,' she admitted. 'Larry's been in one of his moods and that puts me off life altogether. There's a German who should have been in touch with him and hasn't been … I wish sometimes that Larry would …' She stopped.

'Would what?'

'Would persuade me to mind my own business,' she answered, crudely turning aside his question.

He looked inquiringly at her for a time, then led the way into the sitting-room. He asked her what she'd like to drink.

'What I'd really enjoy is a whisky, if that's not being too greedy? I like it so much, even if it is imported and costs the earth.'

'It isn't being greedy and I'll make it a Spanish double to try and cheer you up. How do you like it? On the rocks? With water or soda?'

'I've some not too distant Scottish ancestry so I'll have it with plain water, please.' She sniffed the air. 'This room smells of wine. Have you had a catastrophe and broken a bottle?'

He accepted the explanation she'd given him. 'A total catastrophe. I dropped a bottle of red and had just finished clearing up the mess when you arrived.' He went into the kitchen, picked up the jar of wine and returned it to the larder, poured out their drinks and carried them through.

'Where's Elvina?' she asked casually, as he handed her her drink.

'She felt rather tired when we got back so she decided to go up to bed for a lie-down. She may be down later.'

'I'd like to wait, but I can't be away too long. Larry will want his meal: he doesn't like it as late as the locals have it. Now we haven't got a full-time maid, I have to turn to and do some work for a change.' She spoke in a self-contemptuous manner.

'Why only for a change?'

She played with the glass, twisting it round in her fingers. 'Because I've spent a lot of my life avoiding work. I didn't do anything at school or university, yet somehow managed to scrape a degree, which surprised my tutor not a little. I was going to train to do something useful, but I met a Greek who was very handsome and who suggested we see the world together. My mother said he was a rotter, and for once she was right. When I crept back to my mother she'd married again and I lived with her because my new stepfather was really wealthy, but he seemed to think my bed should be his as well as my mother's. So I moved in with Larry, whom I'd always liked except when in one of his moods. And he's always lived as if he were wealthy, so I still haven't had a regular job.' She looked straight at him. 'Have I shocked you with the sordid family saga?'

'No,' he answered. 'Were you trying to?'

She didn't immediately answer him, but asked for a cigarette. After smoking for a short while, she said: 'You're strange and part of your charm is I can't really make you out. Most of the time you talk and act like the sobersides farmer you claim to be, but then occasionally I get a different impression. I reckon you can be pretty reckless and unconformist ...' She stopped.

He drank. 'Reckless' went some of the way to describing his present actions. 'I'll be conformist and blame my split personality on my parents. My father dreams and paints pictures which usually don't sell very well and my mother is so practical she keeps the home going on the money he doesn't earn.'

'That explains everything except how on earth you became a farmer.'

'Why not? It's one of the most rewarding and exciting jobs one can do.'

'Exciting? You've got to be joking.'

So he told her about tilling the soil and making it yield, the intense satisfaction of harvesting, the endless search for the unattainable — the perfect cow — the thrill when the dipstick of the bulk tank showed an increase in milk against all the odds since drought was burning up the grass and therefore the increase could only be due to expert stockmanship ...

'You damn near make me want to grab a hoe and start hoeing,' she said, clearly surprised by the depth of his enthusiasm.

He grinned. 'Curb the desire — it's hell on the back. You should have stopped me becoming a bore. Elvina says I sound like an overlong wartime exhortation to dig for victory.'

'Never mind what it sounds like: it's constructive instead of destructive, like so much out here.'

'Why don't you go back to England?' he asked quietly.

'To what? And as what? I'm not trained to do anything — I told you that just now. So can you see me as a nine-to-five secretary, ready to uncross my legs every time the boss goes by because he might give me a free dinner and so save my having to eat in some grotty café?'

'No, I can't see you like that. But there must be many jobs where really fluent Spanish will be worth a lot. What I was thinking of was Elvina's description of this place — a lotus island, dangerous to anyone young enough to have an intelligent ambition.'

'Maybe I don't have and don't want an intelligent ambition.'

'Then force yourself to go out and find one.'

'Too late. I've already eaten of the enchanted mushroom, or whatever it was.' She finished her drink. 'I must be moving.'

'Surely you'll have the other half?'

'No, thanks. In the name of health, I never get tight before a meal and you gave me such an enormous first half.' She stood up. 'Sorry to have inflicted myself.'

He smiled at her. 'Is this a case of an intelligent assessment or are you seeking an instant and complimentary rebuttal?'

'Swine,' she answered. 'Four-legged, snorting, large black saddlebag swine.'

He roared with laughter. 'Saddleback, and very good pigs they are.'

'I'll take your word for it ... Drop in and see me, John. We're only a short walk away and although you're obviously a swine of some sort, you do cheer me up.'

He accompanied her to her car and saw her off, then returned back into the house. She'd given him confidence. Clearly, she'd found not the slightest reason to doubt his story that Elvina was upstairs, lying down. So why should anyone else become at all suspicious?

The days passed and yet the cable announcing Maitland's death did not arrive. He began to panic. Surely, he couldn't keep Elvina 'alive' much longer? Yet here, he recognized, her past character and the character of the English Community helped him. Elvina had been forthright, to the point of rudeness at times, and too obviously amused by all the self-conscious, unwritten rules of etiquette. For their part, the English Community were both contemptuous of, and scared of, independence and nonconformity so there had been little real contact between them and, lacking anyone she saw very regularly, her absence was not remarked. No one came to Ca'n Manin to ask what had happened to her and was she ill? If she'd been lying at the foot of the stairs with a broken back, dying from dehydration and starvation, no one would have known. His only real problem was to make Elvina's continued absence reasonable to Catalina. And here the weather helped him. It remained sunny and the temperature kept rising so that it was perfectly reasonable to go out on a constant succession of picnics.

CHAPTER XI

THE CABLE, Lady Eastmore, and José Mayans, arrived within half an hour of each other on Friday morning, nine days after Elvina had died.

A young man on a noisy motor-bike came up the dirt-track at speed, imagining himself a trials champion. Tatham, in the hall when he first heard the noise, stepped out to meet him. He came to a clunking halt and the motor cut out. He reached into the satchel slung round his side, brought out half-a-dozen envelopes and found the one he wanted, asked Tatham to sign the tear-off strip and tore this off. He started the bike's engine, revved wildly, and left, scattering a hail of loose stones as soon as he crossed from the concrete to the dirt-track.

Tatham opened the envelope and read the telegram, which was dated the previous day: GEOFFREY DIED THIS MORNING STOP FUNERAL ON SATURDAY AT THREE PM MADGE

He continued staring at the cable after he'd read it. Elvina had said she'd go to the funeral and Madge most probably knew this. So arrangements must be made to book a flight ticket. Then tonight her 'death' must be arranged — and over the past few days he'd worked out as certainly as possible how to ensure her body was entirely defrosted before it was discovered.

His thoughts were interrupted by the sounds of an approaching car. After the total quiet of the past days, now everyone seemed to be visiting. A Daimler on English plates came round the comer and up the dirt-track and as it passed the estanque he identified the driver as Lady Eastmore. There was someone in the passenger seat.

'Good morning, Mr Tatham. I'd like you to meet a very old friend of mine,' said Lady Eastmore graciously. 'Mrs Wade.' Her graciousness did not extend to Christian names.

He shook hands with Mrs Wade. She was an extraordinary sight. A small, well-proportioned head was set on top of a vast body which grew in bulk as it descended, rather like a female Michelin tyre woman. Incredibly, she wore slacks. It was difficult to know whether to admire her courage or be astonished by the extent of her blind bad taste.

'Mrs Wade flew over last night,' said Lady Eastmore. 'From her seat in Oxfordshire.'

And the rest of her stretched a long way, too, he thought.

'It was a shocking flight,' said the mountain, in a deep, rolling, cavernous voice. 'Very uncomfortable. And the meal was so frugal.'

How on earth had they fitted her in, he wondered?

'We'd like to have a word with Elvina,' said Lady East-more. 'Is she in?'

'No, I'm afraid she isn't. She went out not long before you arrived.'

Lady Eastmore looked at the Fiat in the lean-to garage.

'For a walk,' he said. 'She's probably gone up the valley.'

'I'd no idea she liked walking. Will she be a long time?'

'I don't really know.' Why the questions? he wondered. And why the visit? 'Why not have a cup of coffee and she might return before you have to leave.'

'That is an idea,' said Lady Eastmore. 'Norah, shall we sit outside? It's really warm enough.'

'I should think so,' replied the mountain dubiously, as she looked at the rather narrow-seated garden chairs.

Make yourselves at home, he thought. He went into the hall and brought out one of the wood and leather chairs which were considerably wider than the garden chairs. The mountain omitted to thank him and lowered herself. There was sufficient displacement of flesh to allow her to settle.

He went into the kitchen and made coffee, poured it into a jug which he placed on a tray, together with cups, saucers, spoons, sugar, milk, and half-a-dozen biscuits. Seconds after putting the tray down outside on the garden table, a bejewelled hand reached out and plucked a biscuit off the table. The mountain began to eat, pausing only to ask for five spoonfuls of sugar in her coffee.

'Quite a nice little place your aunt has here,' said Lady Eastmore, in the tones of one who could afford to be generous because any comparison with her own house was ludicrous. 'Of course, it would have been very much nicer if it hadn't been converted by a Mallorquin. Their tastes are so pedestrian.'

There was a silence, which he made no effort to break. Had Elvina been due to visit the Eastmores the previous evening? But she'd said nothing about any forthcoming date, which surely she would have done over an event as unlikely as that? And it was impossible to believe Lady Eastmore would call on anyone the day after that person had rudely failed to honour an invitation.

Lady Eastmore drank some coffee. 'How are you enjoying it on our island?' she finally asked, a note of annoyance in her voice because he had not the wit to conduct a social conversation.

'It's quite pleasant, but I'll be glad to return home.'

'He farms,' said Lady Eastmore, to the mountain. The mountain swivelled round and examined him more closely. 'Whereabouts do you farm, Mr Tatham?'

'Right now, I don't any more. I relinquished the lease before coming out here.'

'Really.' The mountain reached for another biscuit. 'We have a few farms,' she said, without any emphasis.

He could imagine it. Thousands of very profitable acres, expertly managed, and no more to her or her husband than figures on a balance sheet.

Lady Eastmore opened her crocodile-skin handbag and brought out a slim gold cigarette-case. She offered it to the mountain, helped herself to one of the cigarettes. 'I'm sure you wouldn't like one of our women's cigarettes,' she said, shutting the case and denying him the chance of finding out for himself. 'We have them flown out from home. The Spanish simply have no idea how to make a decent cigarette.'

Was there anything in Spain which suited her? He flicked open his lighter for them.

As he lit one of his own cigarettes, a dirty, dented Citroen 2CV came rattling round the corner and up the dirt-track. It parked close to the spotless, gleaming Daimler. Mayans, smiling broadly, forty-eight hours' stubble on his chin, shirt unbuttoned to show much of his hairy chest, trousers streaked with dirt, stepped out and came across to where they sat. He spoke rapidly and at some length in Spanish. Tatham waited for Lady Eastmore to translate.

'He has been eating an inordinate amount of garlic,' she said.

'Terrible stuff for humans, good for horses,' said the mountain. 'Had a damn good hunter once which fell ill and the vet couldn't do anything with it. Fool man — came from up north somewhere. I crushed up a dozen cloves of garlic in some bran with castor oil and fed it and that hunter ran round the paddock as if it was at The Oaks.'

'The flavour can be pleasant, if it's only a hint,' said Lady Eastmore, 'but these people will chew the stuff. We had a maid once whom I caught chewing some whilst she was making my bed. She claimed it was to help ward off the evil eye. They are riddled with ridiculous superstitions.' Mayans stared with growing surprise from one woman to the other. It was inconceivable to him, not having had the advantage of their highly educated background, that they could be rudely ignoring what he'd said, yet he couldn't think why no one was answering him.

Tatham said: 'Would you mind telling me what he wants?'

Lady Eastmore looked slightly annoyed. 'He's asking to speak to your aunt. The impertinence of these people is quite incredible. No hesitation in interrupting us.'

'Could you tell him she's out at the moment, so if it's not urgent he'd better come back tomorrow … No, that's no good because she'll be flying home. If he …'

'You say Elvina is returning to England?' said Lady Eastmore. 'Why?'

Her peremptory question angered him, but his manner remained cordial. 'Her godfather's just died and she was very fond of him so she's going to the funeral.'

'You are talking about Geoffrey Maitland?' asked the mountain.

'Yes, that's right. Did you know him?'

'My husband was acquainted with him. An extraordinary man.' She grabbed the last biscuit. 'Quarrelled with everyone, especially his relatives. I heard he'd died, just before I left yesterday. Very wealthy, but quite impossible.'

'I believe Elvina was fairly close to him?' asked Lady Eastmore.

'I think she was, yes,' replied Tatham.

'She mentioned once that as his goddaughter …'

Tatham, meant to pick up the sentence and complete it, didn't. He could imagine the puckish delight with which Elvina would have hinted at the possibility of her inheriting a fortune. No wonder Lady Eastmore had hurried round to try to discover the truth. Elvina comfortably off but not rich was one thing, Elvina very rich was another. A denial of the right and natural order of things. A threat to the Community. An invitation to her not to know her proper station.

Mayans, his smile now very laboured, gestured with his hands as he spoke again.

Lady Eastmore didn't bother to look at him as she snapped out a few words.

'Is he …?' began Tatham.

'The wretched man is still inquiring where Elvina is and demanding to speak to her. I told him she wasn't here and she was leaving for England and that he should have the manners not to interrupt us. I find his Castilian accent atrocious and his Mallorquin is a mumble. Does he suffer from some speech defect?'

'Not as far as I know,' said Tatham.

'Then he should take the trouble to speak his own languages distinctly. Sheer laziness, as always.'

Mayans, finally realizing the last word had been spoken, turned and left and went back to his car, more puzzled than outraged.

Lady Eastmore slid back the cover of her gold Rolex and checked the time. The large solitaire diamond — diamonds were so useful in times of currency crises — glinted in the sun. 'Norah, I think we can wait no longer, or we shall have almost no time at all in Palma. It really is incredible, isn't it, Mr Tatham, that in a so-called capital city the shops should all close for three hours at lunch-time. Really, one would have imagined by now that they'd have discovered a little business sense.' She stood up. The mountain started to follow suit, but the chair had become stuck to her enormous buttocks and it began to follow her up. She hit the chair with clenched fists and knocked it off herself. Her composure remained complete.

They said goodbye, briefly and slightly patronizingly. Tatham held open the passenger door and the mountain shuffled herself into the Daimler, causing it to list when she finally settled.

'Tell Elvina we called,' commanded Lady Eastmore, just before she shut the door. She started the engine, put the selection handle to reverse, backed with expert judgment, and drove down the dirt-track.

He went through to the kitchen and packed the freezy-bag for another picnic. He put five hundred pesetas in a used envelope and stuck this on the window over the sink for Catalina. That done, he collected travellers' cheques and passport from his bedroom, made a final check that the deep-freeze remained locked — he'd lost count how many times he'd done this — and went out with the freezy-bag and the wine to the Fiat.

Elvina's bank was in Puerto Llueso, on the small square and at right-angles to the church. The assistant manager — one of three men who worked at the bank — recognized him and smiled a greeting, asked in broken English how he and Mrs Woods were, then cashed travellers' cheques for a hundred pounds after a brief look at his passport.

He drove to the travel agents, whose place was on the Llueso road just back from the front. He asked for a ticket to London on the following morning for Mrs Woods and explained it was at such short notice because of an unexpected death: would they see if it could possibly be arranged. The girl behind the counter, understanding far more English than she spoke, said she'd do what she could to help and would he return in half an hour's time to find out the answer.

He walked the short distance to the harbour and went along the western arm. Many yachts and motor-cruisers were tied up, bow or stem on, and he noticed how high a proportion of the larger ones were flying the red duster or the flag of one of the better-known English yacht clubs: no wonder, he thought, it was difficult to persuade the average Mallorquin that not all English were millionaires. The light breeze was slapping halliards against masts with the sharp evocative sounds that were found in all harbours around the world.

On the bay side of the arm, there was a two-metre-high wall, built in two stages. He climbed this and gazed out at the bay. Blue water, lighter blue, cloudless sky, grey-green mountains. A medium-sized yacht, with spinnaker in red and blue stripes, sailed past. A power-boat, 120 h.p. outboard churning the water white, sped across towards the air force base, towing a water-skier who was criss-crossing the wake. Suppose, he thought, Maitland's money eventually did come to him. He could buy a farm, work all hours, and make a lot less money than if he invested the capital, did nothing, and lived on the interest. Why not live here, in luxury? He rejected the idea. This *was* lotus island: initiative and ambition were killed so subtly that the victim didn't realize it until too late. He couldn't be happy doing nothing. In any case, Elvina wanted a memorial of green, fertile fields.

The travel agency said Mrs Woods was lucky. Because the season was not really under way, they'd been able to book her on the next morning's flight to Heathrow. The ticket cost 8,300 pesetas. He paid the money and thanked the girl for all her help and she smiled and answered in traditional style that it was nothing.

He drove along the front road, past all the bars where everything cost at least twice as much as two roads back, past hotels still mostly shut, and turned on to the Parelona road which wound a tortuous way over the mountains, offering dramatic views, and down to the justly famous Parelona beach where the sands really did seem more golden and the water bluer than anywhere else on the island.

Roughly half-way to Parelona, on top of the mountains, was a parking area and viewing point, the latter out on a small peninsula of rock with sheer faces which swept dizzily down to the sea: a magnificent but vertiginous place. He parked the car and climbed out.

There was a path up and out to the actual viewing-point platform and this had rails, but, typically, the cliff edge on either side stretched away without any protection whatsoever. It would be relatively simple to roll the body over the edge at almost any point, though the left-hand side was the better because it was flatter and more regular. After a body had fallen from such a height, all signs of previous injuries would be lost forever.

*

The telephone rang and Ingham answered it. Judy watched his expression and was very thankful when she saw him smile and heard his voice lighten as he began to speak German. She understood nothing, but caught the name Naupert. Then the Germans hadn't pulled right out of the house sale.

She lit a cigarette. She knew Lawrence was engaged in some sort of trickery, guessed it was centred around the painting on the far wall, but took care not to find out anything more. If she discovered for certain he was swindling someone, she would leave: all the time she only suspected he was, she'd stay. Her attitude was hypocritical, but she accepted the fact that she was a hypocrite.

She could still vividly recall the near-poverty that had followed the death of her father, could still mentally cringe at the sense of personal degradation of being taken to relations who were asked for 'loans'. The change when her mother had married Lawrence had been dramatic. Suddenly, a decent school, home became a succession of large houses, with servants to do the work, in different parts of the Continent, life became the art of seeking pleasure. Spyridon, the dilettante poet, taught her that love was beautiful but, like all things, it needed freedom if it was to continue to flower. The man-made status of marriage destroyed freedom and strangled love. So much nonsense when one had reached maturity, heady stuff for one discovering the world. Spyridon had been a right royal bastard. He'd thought she was wealthy in her own right. When he'd discovered the truth, he'd left her, penniless, stranded, to seek better and more secure prospects to whom he could whisper his poems of love. Bloody awful poems. She'd returned to her mother, now married to Jacques, suffered endless recriminations of the I-told-you-so pattern, and settled in. Jacques had been a clever bastard. He'd flattered her, but so carefully he'd lulled her native shrewdness and he'd taken her by complete surprise when he'd invaded her bedroom whilst her mother was away for three days in England. She'd hit a trifle too hard in a delicate area and it had taken Jacques a long time to recover physically: his pride never made a full recovery. On her return, her mother was horrified. All right, Jacques should have kept to his own bed, but couldn't she have shown a glimmer of discretion? There were more ways of dealing with a randy man (when he was rich) than hitting him in his family jewels. So she left that house. She asked if she could stay a while with Lawrence, whom she'd always liked, and Lawrence had immediately invited her to stay with him on a permanent basis. Since then, she'd been happy yet discontented, worrying because to him honesty was a word of elastic definition whilst to her it was not, slightly contemptuous of herself because she lacked the courage — if that was the right word — to make her own way in life.

Ingham replaced the receiver. 'That was some officious secretary of Naupert's telling me two surveyors will arrive tomorrow and would I please give them every facility to make their inspection. And had I considered the asking price further?'

'To which you answered?'

'Not a peseta less than twenty million.' He went over to the door of the bar, opened it, and went inside.

'I thought you always let a purchaser knock the price down a little to make him feel good?'

'Not this time, Judy, not this time.' He came out of the bar with two glasses and handed her one in which was a gin and tonic. He sat down on the settee. 'This time, Herr Naupert is going to feel more than good even without knocking the price down one single pfennig.'

She stopped herself wondering why. 'Would you rather I went out tomorrow?'

'Good heavens, why? It can't possibly matter if you're here.'

It was a lovely house, she thought, the kind of house she would give much to own. But it wasn't worth twenty million. So why was Lawrence so certain the German — 'the smartest, hardest bastard in Germany today' — would pay something like five million more than it was currently worth? She found she was asking herself the question she had determined not to ask herself.

*

Marie Mayans finely chopped up tomatoes, onions, peppers (very expensive, still), and a clove of garlic, and dropped them into the warm olive oil in the frying-pan. She stirred the mixture.

'Señora Woods was out,' said Mayans. He poured himself a brandy.

She crossed the small kitchen to the table, pushing past him with more force than was necessary. She began to scrape off the flesh from the two cooked hindlegs of a rabbit.

'But I will persuade her.' He stared quickly at her, then pounded the table with his fist.

She did not look up from her task as she said, using a picturesque Mallorquin phrase, that many unlikely things would have to happen before the English señora would pay a single peseta more than the rent agreed to by a man whose brain had been addled by cognac.

He became almost tearfully indignant. 'But when she signed the contract, it was a wonderful rent. It was more than anyone else was getting.'

She pushed past him again as she carried the rabbit meat to the stove and dropped it into the frying-pan. She stirred the mixture, then added a little more oil.

'I'll show you,' he shouted, 'that I know what to do.'

'You'll show me how to drink. And how to talk. But not how to make money.'

'If we sell that field to the Dutchman ...'

'Bring him here so that I can talk to him.'

'No,' he muttered sulkily, 'he'll only do business with a man ... Marie, he's offering two million pesetas. Two whole million.' He thought about the figure and poured himself another drink.

'You're not doing any more business for me until that English señora is paying a proper rent for my house: not if the Dutchman offers ten million.'

Dolores entered the kitchen, looked at Mayans, and giggled. He cursed her and suggested that, despite her mode of life, her mother had been insensible to shame. He drank the brandy with angry haste.

'Dolores,' said Marie, 'cut the bread and put some oil on it and stop giggling.'

Dolores went past Mayans, swinging her hips and sending her mini skirt fluttering because she knew he couldn't keep his eyes off a good pair of thighs. She cut three slices of pan Mallorquin, poured olive oil on to them, sprinkled them with salt, and put them on three plates.

*

'That young man,' said the mountain, 'didn't seem to know Geoffrey Maitland, did he, Mary?' She reached over to the glass dish of salted peanuts, picked up several and hurried them to her mouth. She chewed quickly and swallowed, reached out and picked up several more. She spoke before she ate them. 'His estate will be a fairly large one. He bought a lot of land for investment several years ago and I was told some of it is very likely to get planning permission.'

Lord Eastmore tried not to look as bored as he felt and fidgeted with his cigar.

'It seems,' went on the mountain, after swallowing, 'from what you say about Elvina Woods that it's a very great pity she is probably going to inherit.'

Lady Eastmore sipped her white Cinzano with a dash of soda. The mountain, annoyed with the waste of time, picked up the glass dish and emptied the contents into the palm of her left hand. In between much more rapid mouthfuls, she said: 'Charles, did you say there was some nasty little snooper from the Bank of England going round this place, checking up on bank accounts and all that sort of thing?'

'So I've been told.'

'Fellow ought to be hanged. That would teach him to mind his own business. We've gone far too soft ... Mary, have you a few more peanuts? I rather enjoy one or two with a drink. And if it's not too much trouble, I'd like another drink. This heat makes me very thirsty.' She suddenly belched, but with the gentility of generations of good breeding.

CHAPTER XII

WHEN IT WAS dark — and the night was very dark because at sunset the clouds, dramatically edged with red, had come rolling in from the north-east — Tatham went into the garage and lowered the back seat of the Fiat to provide the full cargo compartment.

Back in the house, he collected together four of the plastic boxes, filled with cotton-wool, that Elvina always had with her when flower-hunting, her camera with special lens, the book on flowers of South-West Europe, a torch, and her handbag. He checked on flowers peculiar to Mallorca and picked out *Scutellaria balearica*, which he underlined with ink and against which he put a question mark, which had been her way of identifying species she was specifically seeking.

Lifting out the body from the deep-freeze was not as unpleasant a task as he had imagined it might be. The bedspread was still firmly secured around her and in any case he was soon suffering from hands so cold it was impossible to worry about much else. He placed the body in the cargo compartment of the Fiat.

On the front passenger seat he put flower book, open at the relevant page, collecting boxes, camera, torch, and her handbag in which was the cable from Madge which had given news of Maitland's death and the ticket to London. He returned to the house and collected a second torch, slim enough to fit into his pocket, a pair of gloves, and a large sheet of brown paper, together with a long length of string.

He switched off all the lights except the one in the hall and up in his bedroom, locked the front door, and climbed into the car. The drive to Puerto Llueso and then on along the Parelona road was totally uneventful, with very little traffic even in the Puerto. There was no other car in the parking area by the viewing point.

Potentially, the greatest moment of danger had always clearly been when he was crossing from the car to the edge of the cliff. But this distance was only a few metres and because the road was uphill from either direction any approaching car — necessarily in an intermediate gear and revving hard — would be audible and its headlights visible long before the occupants would be in a position to note him.

He backed the Fiat so that the tailgate was towards the sea, switched off the lights, and waited, with both windows down. He heard the murmur of the wind across the stunted scrub and grass and the distant hiss of the sea below as the small waves beat against the rock faces. Then he heard a car approaching from the Parelona direction and seconds later he saw the reflection of the headlights, though not the lights themselves. He counted. After approximately forty-five seconds, the car breasted the road and gathered speed along the hundred-metre stretch of level to the descent and the first left-hand turn. Because the Fiat was set back from the road, the headlights had at no time been focused directly on it or even very near it. He waited and a few minutes later a car approached from the Puerto direction. This one took thirty-three seconds to come into view. Then he had a minimum of thirty-three seconds in which to get from the Fiat to the cliff edge.

He climbed out of the car — he'd previously taped the light buttons so that the interior lights did not automatically come on — and made a last audible and visual check: he heard and saw nothing. He went round to the rear, lifted up the tailgate, slid the body back until he could lift it out. Then, at no small effort, he hooked his elbow over the tailgate and slammed this shut.

He heard a car approaching from the Parelona direction.

His eyes were well attuned to the dark and he could just make out the edge of the cliff. He began to walk and almost immediately stumbled badly as his right foot caught in an unseen pothole. He cursed, but did not dare use a torch.

He had counted thirty by the time he reached the edge of the cliff. He knelt and the wind, damped from the sea, came up vertically to ruffle his face. He undid the cover and rolled the body out, making certain the shoes scraped along the rock. There was a quick rattle of stones, a thud a very short while afterwards, and then silence. The average sea temperature at this time of the year was fifteen degrees centigrade, fractionally more than the air temperature: the body would be thawed out evenly and quite quickly.

Headlights speared the sky and then descended as the car breasted the rise. By then, he was lying down on his stomach, facing the sea, with the Fiat giving him extra cover.

The car passed abreast of him, engine note dropping as the driver changed gear. It gathered speed. Just before it went out of sight, its brake lights shone bright red as the driver prepared for the first corner.

Tatham stood up and returned to the Fiat. He wrapped up the bedcover in the brown paper, tied it up with string and added a loop so that he could carry it over his shoulders. He set the rear car-seat back in position and checked no traces were left.

It was going to be a long walk. But he was used to hard physical exercise and at another time he would have enjoyed it. By happy chance, the old mule track between Puerto Llueso and Parelona, built centuries before, crossed at the same point as the road so that they ran for a while parallel to each other. He began to walk along the track, using the torch when absolutely necessary as it zigzagged to avoid too steep a gradient. Above him or below him, up to a kilometre away at times, the occasional car passed by, covering in minutes a journey that was going to take him hours.

CHAPTER XIII

ENRIQUE ALVAREZ PALASI was both an anomaly and an enigma. He was an anomaly because members of the Cuerpo de Policia were supposed to work from police stations belonging to the Policia Armada y de Tráfico: he was an enigma because none of his companions could understand him. In the Llueso station of the Guardia Civil he was known as The Loner and the captain in charge of the sector had sworn to get rid of him, but all requests for his transfer clearly became lost between Llueso and Palma for there were never any orders detailing him to move. Had the captain been sufficiently interested, which he wasn't, to discover why Alvarez was around, he would have learned that he'd temporarily been billeted on the Llueso Guardia Civil six years previously because of a sudden and dramatic increase in crime. This had been due to the rowdy behaviour of people who'd come out on a series of holidays organized by an English soccer club's supporters' club. The supporters' club had learned their lesson and never organized another holiday, but no one in Palma thought to give the order to recall Alvarez. Of course, had he been a man of the slightest ambition, he would have set about having himself transferred back from Llueso. But he had none, other than to retire, buy a small patch of land, and sit on this and feel the soil running through his fingers. He'd once said this to a lst-class guard with whom he'd become almost friendly and the 1st-class guard had called him shallow-witted.

He was from peasant stock and proud of the fact. His parents had been illiterate, but good farmers, managing to make a bare living out of three hectares of boulder-strewn land — the other fifteen hectares they'd owned had been pine-woods, incapable of growing crops. Towards the end of the Civil War, his father had been called up and sent to the Peninsula to fight. He'd been wounded, decorated for bravery, and returned. His wound to his back had made farming both difficult and painful and his wife had had to do the hardest work — as she had when he was away. As strong as an ox, and about as graceful, a woman of fierce love and pride, she'd burned herself out in the service of her family.

His parents had been so proud of their only son that no sacrifice had been too great, no work too hard, to give him a better chance in life than ever they'd had. Although illiterate, they'd viewed the future with some understanding and seen things were going to change: so they'd made him go to school before this was obligatory and paid the fees with money that could have bought them just a little comfort in life. He had been a bright pupil.

The tourist boom had started at about the time that his father's back had become considerably worse and his mother had suffered a crippling rheumatism. They'd known very little about the boom until the day an Englishman, round, pleasant face, always smiling, very chatty, had visited their farm and interrupted their sowing. Their land, he'd said, was on the sea and was becoming quite valuable. This had astonished them because pine-woods had never been of any commercial value except, possibly, for making very poor quality charcoal. He could, he went on, get them a really good price for their land and with that money they could buy a proper farm in the plains and grow the kind of crops which until now they'd only dreamed about. What true peasant could ignore such an offer? Of course, the Englishman had added, there would have to be a lot of bargaining with hard-headed businessmen and who better than himself to do the bargaining on their behalf? He'd see no one swindled them. Even in their restricted lives, the saying 'An Englishman's word' had meaning. So with simple faith they'd trusted him, and with simple trickery he'd swindled them, paying them only what the land had been worth as farmland and pine-woods. The Englishman had made so much money on the deal that he'd given large sums to charity and become well known and respected as a philanthropist.

His parents had died shortly afterwards. Take a peasant away from the land and he's no reason for living.

For several years after the death of his parents, he'd stayed with relatives who lived near the fastest-growing strip of tourist land east of Palma. He'd discovered, to his great pleasure, that all the stories about foreign girls were true.

Then, after doing his military training, he'd met Juana-Marie. Juana-Marie was more beautiful than the moon over the water on a summer's night, sweeter than the honey of the wild bees who worked in the foothills of the Sierra de Allabia, more loving than a mother with her firstborn. Every flash of her dark eyes, every toss of her black hair, every smile of her curving lips, gathered up his heart a little more. She was unique and wonderful. She wanted him to become a great person in life. So he forgot the shiftless life he had been living and studied for the competitive exams of the Civil Service. He'd passed, very well. He'd entered the State Police Training School and had come second in his class. A very bright future lay ahead of him.

At five-fifteen one Thursday afternoon, Juana-Marie had left her parents' house to walk to her cousins' who were helping her prepare everything for her wedding. At five-twenty, Robert Jouanier, French, wealthy, had decided to go out and buy more wine. His current girlfriend tried to dissuade him, saying he'd drunk too much to go anywhere, but he was at the stage where any opposition, however reasonable, merely stiffened his drunken intentions. He took a very sharp corner at 60 k.p.h. and lost control of his Mercedes. It mounted the pavement and pinned Juana-Marie against a wall and she died quite quickly.

Alvarez lost all his ambition.

*

The guard, grey-green jacket off because the day was warm and the building old and stuffy, put his head round Alvarez's door. 'Hey, wake up. There's work for you.'

Alvarez looked up from the book he'd been reading. 'You make it sound like there's been an earthquake.' He was squat, broad-shouldered, and had a heavy face that tended to become owlish in expression when he wore horn-rimmed glasses, which he did for reading small print. His complexion was dark, yet in his features there was no strong hint of Moorish ancestors.

The guard grimaced. 'One tremor and I'll guarantee you wouldn't just be sitting there …! There's a foreigner been along to the Municipal boys to say his aunt seems to be missing.'

'So what am I supposed to do? Pluck her out of the air?'

'You're a bad-tempered old sod,' said the guard, just before he left and shut the door.

Alvarez wasn't bad-tempered, just indifferently cynical. Foreigners were always going missing. Usually one found them in bed with a member of the opposite sex: sometimes of the same sex. Age seemed to be no bar. He'd once tracked down a man of seventy-one who'd taken off.

He lit a cheap cigar and stared down at the paper he'd been reading. Real Mallorca were signing on a new and well-known player for the coming season. They'd need more than one new player if they were to get anywhere, judging by the previous year. He'd lost a hundred pesetas over them last season, betting they'd be in the top four of their division.

He picked up the telephone receiver and asked for the Municipal Police and eventually he was put through to them. An Englishman, John Tatham, had been in to say his aunt had not slept at her house the previous night, her car was not in the garage, and she was due to fly to England in less than two hours' time. Her address was in La Huerta. He replaced the receiver. La Huerta was where all the foreign money lived. Much of that money had been made out of land on the island. Lots of people said the foreigners were a good thing because their money had brought prosperity to the island: who now saw children bare-footed in the streets? But couldn't shoes have been provided without prostituting the land?

He left the building by one of the side doors and walked along the narrow street to the square and the Llueso Club. In the bar, he ordered a coffee and a brandy. He lit a cigarette and studied his reflection in the mirror. A brooding face, a crumpled shirt because no woman ironed for him, a tie because regulations demanded it and not even he could ignore them too blatantly all the time, the top button of his shirt undone because he hated any restraint around his bull neck. When the precious, wealthy young Englishman in La Huerta saw him, there'd be a delicate raised eyebrow: no one could look so bloody superior as the English. But he didn't give a sparrow's fart for any Englishman. He'd ship the lot home in a Civil War prisoner-of-war hulk, to see what that did to their exquisite manners.

The waiter moved along the counter to pass him his coffee and cognac. 'You look like you've just lost the ticket that won the lottery,' said the waiter.

'It's my indigestion.'

'My doctor says that anyone with indigestion should immediately give up drinking coffee and cognac.'

'I'll keep belching.'

A man farther along the counter laughed. 'Can't you see, Alberto, he knows you're fiddling the duros but is killing himself trying to find out how.'

'When I decide to pinch the pesetas,' boasted the waiter, 'I'll not mess around with duros.'

Alvarez stirred sugar into his coffee. 'Does anyone know whereabouts in La Huerta Ca'n Manin is?'

'Ca'n Manin?' The waiter leaned both elbows on the bar. 'Is that where the American millionaire lives who brings a new wife from America each year?'

'It's an Englishwoman who's got a nephew staying with her right now.'

'I know,' said the man down the bar. 'It's not in the urbanization, but up on the road to the castle and past that big house which looks like somebody had a bad dream. It belongs to José.' He chuckled. 'Or his wife. The old Englishwoman who lives there is clever and mad.'

'A useful combination,' said Alvarez, as he drank some brandy.

'Too clever for José — that's for sure. She signed a lifelong lease at a rent which must make her laugh every time she thinks about it. José's wife beats him over the head and calls him names no lady should know because for a stupid foreigner the rent now should be over ten thousand a month.'

'And why is she mad?'

'Why is anyone mad? God and women make them that way. My cousin works for the English and she has heard them say that the señora from Ca'n Manin is mad.'

Alvarez finished the brandy and then the coffee. He paid — two five-peseta pieces, which the man along the bar loudly said Alberto would pocket as soon as Alvarez was out of sight.

Alvarez's car was parked near the Guardia Civil station, close by one of the schools. It was a beaten-up Seat 600, held together by bits of wire and the skill of the garage. One day he'd have to buy another. One day.

He hated La Huerta. A concentration of expensive modern houses and bungalows, the old fincas with but few exceptions taken over and rebuilt to the point where they bore little resemblance to what they'd been, the displacement of many of the farmers because not even the most skilful and intensive market gardening could equal the profit of selling land to the foreigners, the ghastly urbanización with the houses crawling up the sides of the mountain and debasing it, the large cars on national or tourist plates whose owners were not forced to pay the luxury taxes that all Spaniards had to …

Ca'n Manin initially surprised him because its exterior at the front had not been altered, except to fit glass windows in place of solid wooden shutters. Then he remembered it was still owned by a Mallorquin. He parked by the side of the empty lean-to garage and climbed out. Even in his present disgruntled mood he had to enjoy the setting: the small garden, the orange grove, the loquats bright with fruits almost ripe, the almond trees with well-formed nuts, the monastery mountain, Puig Llueso, the distant bay ...

A man came out of the house. Not at all the kind of man he had expected. This one had the air of honest physical work and open air about him and his clothes didn't look as though they'd come from a boutique.

Tatham introduced himself. Alvarez, who'd learned English partly from all the girls he'd known before he met Juana-Marie, partly from more formal teachers because a man who was going to be really important in the world needed to speak good English, said: 'Inspector Alvarez of the Cuerpo General de Policia. Or, as you would say, the CID.' His accent was good.

'I do hope I'm not bothering you unnecessarily.'

The English, he thought, were always apologizing: as they kicked you where it most hurt, they apologized politely for doing it.

'But I'm really worried. My aunt didn't sleep in her bed last night, nor has she turned up to get ready to fly back to England.' Tatham looked at his watch. 'As a matter of fact, she's too late now. She can't possibly catch the plane.'

'May we sit down somewhere and you will tell me all that has happened from the beginning?'

'Of course. Would you prefer inside or outside?'

'Outside, if you don't mind.' He wasn't going to be outdone in the politeness stakes.

'Will you have something to drink?'

'I would like, please, a small cognac.'

Tatham left. Alvarez sat down on one of the small metal garden chairs and stared out across the garden and through the chestnut and pomegranate trees at the orange grove. His parents should have had a place like this, if the proper money had been paid to them. His father could have rested his sore back and his mother her worn-out body and they could have employed someone whom they'd have watched till the soil and grow three or four fine crops a year.

Tatham returned as two quick explosions — they were blasting out foundations at the back for a new house-thudded through the air and echoed briefly against the surrounding mountains. The brandy, Alvarez immediately recognized, was something like Don Carlos and not the Fundador he usually had. All the good things in the country went to the foreigners. He lit a cigar, asked for details of the missing woman, made a few notes in his book, and inquired whether the house had a telephone. It had.

The sitting-room was large, very high-ceilinged, and attractive. So the foreigners didn't have a monopoly on good taste! The telephone was on a small corner cupboard and he lifted the receiver and when the exchange answered asked for the airport. The operator said there was an hour's delay to the airport. He identified himself and was speaking to the airport inside seven minutes. Iberia Flight IB 501 had been called, all the passengers had been taken by bus to the plane, the plane would be leaving in under five minutes, and according to the passenger lists one passenger had failed to report, but they'd no idea at the moment what was the name of that passenger.

He returned to the patio. 'It seems probable Señora Woods did not join the plane. I will make inquiries. Will you, please, inform me immediately if the señora returns here?'

'Yes, of course.'

He left, driving away in the squeaky Seat. If he felt even more disgruntled than when he'd arrived it was, he was honest enough to admit, because the Englishman had not been a tailor's dummy with squeaky voice and over-smooth hands, smoking scented cigarettes in a holder. Very annoying.

*

It had all gone off so much more easily that Tatham had imagined it would. The detective — he'd looked as if he'd slept in his clothes — had seemed unsurprised that Elvina should be missing and had almost shrugged his shoulders at the possibility of catastrophe's overtaking her while she was searching for some flowers she'd been told might be in the area. But then this was the land of the mañanas. Never do anything that it isn't absolutely essential to do, never look for trouble and if it insists on staring you in the face, step round it. If Elvina's body was washed ashore somewhere it was going to seem quite obvious that she had fallen down the cliff while plant-hunting. Why trouble to seek any other solution to her death?

There was one thing he had not done — re-stock the deep-freeze. Since the only place he knew off-hand which had a deep-freeze was the supermarket in the Puerto, he must hire a car and drive down there.

He walked into Llueso, crossing the Roman bridge over the Torrente Ebrar, now no more than a thin trickle of water, and went along the Calle de la Huerta, past houses which looked empty because their shutters were mostly closed, down past the church to the square, and through to the old football pitch (now the dry-goods market-place on a Sunday) and the garage where Elvina always took her car for servicing. He spoke to the owner, who said something about Señora Woods. When he didn't understand, the other roared with laughter. So different from most countries, thought Tatham, where one's lack of understanding of the native tongue was treated with contempt. He showed his driving licence, signed a form he didn't understand, paid the two days' rent of six hundred pesetas, and drove off in a Seat 600.

The supermarket was busy. Women — mostly English — pushed around wire trolleys or carried wire baskets and gossiped while the few men collected by the long shelves stocked with drink and, for the most part in silence, walked slowly up and down as they studied prices. He loaded his trolley with packets of frozen food selected at random and the bill was 2,400 pesetas.

When he returned to Ca'n Manin, he carried the two cardboard boxes through to the wash-room and emptied the food into the deep-freeze. He was surprised to find it was very much less full than it had been. But this was a point of no importance. He left the lid unlocked.

CHAPTER XIV

CATALINA WAS a handsome woman in her late thirties, dark-skinned, jet black hair, a long face with regular, determined features. She worked in the mornings for one English family down in the Puerto and in the afternoons for Elvina. She spoke no English, yet she understood a little provided it was simple and spoken slowly: in turn, she would speak a simple Spanish and make very expressive use of her hands.

As on every weekday, she arrived by bicycle at Ca'n Manin at three o'clock — an elastic three o'clock — in the afternoon. Tatham was sitting out on the patio and after leaving her bicycle leaning against the side of the garage, she walked up to him and asked him, with a cheerful smile, how he was. He said he was very well, but the Señora Woods was missing.

She put down the canvas bag in which she carried an apron and her expression was now one of concern. Was the señora not well?

'I don't know. She is not here.' He pointed to the house and shook his head.

She understood that, but not what lay behind the fact. Her luxuriant black eyebrows rose in questioning surprise. Where was the señora if she wasn't in the house?

He tried to tell her in French, since there was so often a similarity between that language and Mallorquin, but she shook her head. He went into the hall. On a shelf running along the outer wall between the large fireplace and the outer doors were many of Elvina's reference books. He picked out the English/Spanish dictionary and returned outside. After a while, he was able to explain that Elvina was missing and had not returned to the house the previous night. However, he'd told the police and they would find her.

Catalina, frowning slightly as if not certain she had understood correctly, nodded and said that the police would soon find the señora and the señora would be well.

She picked up her bag and went through to the kitchen. In the next two hours she 'dusted' the house-in true Mallorquin fashion this meant flapping the dust away from where it had previously been — washed down all the floors, swept the patio and washed that down, picked some flowers, and did the little washing up there was. Any English daily woman, contemptuous of the lazy Spaniards, would have considered herself grossly overworked if asked to do that much in a full eight-hour day.

She left at a quarter past five, after expressing the hope that the señora would soon be back in the house. He watched her bicycle down the dirt-track and was quite certain she'd not the slightest idea that Elvina had been dead for ten days.

*

Alvarez lived with remote cousins of his in Calle Juan Rives. The street was four hundred metres long and it had at the far end an olive press, once worked by a blinkered donkey, that was still used by the small-holders of the district. The houses abutted the pavements and were nearly all joined together and in England they would have been called terrace houses, but here, by the use of brightly coloured exteriors and because everywhere was so clean, the total effect from the outside was one of cheerfulness, not sordid poverty. Inside, the houses were even more attractive since each had a small courtyard to give every room sun and in which flowers bloomed all the year round. He had a back bedroom, ate with the family whenever at home for meals, and sat with them in the sitting-room which had once been the stable for a donkey. He was part of the family and yet not part of it, because he refused to let the wife do his washing or mend his clothes or things like that, nor did he spend much time in the sitting-room on the grounds of not being more of a nuisance than he had to be. In fact, he was seeking independence at the same time as he gratefully forwent independence by living with them. There were two children in the house, a boy and a girl, and he spoiled them shamelessly and occasionally to the annoyance of their mother. They were the only people to whom he now dared give his whole affection.

He ate supper at home — soup, dirty rice (rice, peppers, tomatoes, onions, garlic, and a very little chicken), and a sectioned orange — then left the house. He strolled through the narrow twisting streets, stopping for five minutes to discuss local matters with an old woman of eighty, almost blind, who spent every day possible on a chair in the road immediately outside her front door. He reached the square and the club.

Llueso Club was almost a second home to him: it was here he mostly came when, had he been truly part of the cousin's family, he would have relaxed in the sitting-room and watched the very poor-quality television.

Several men greeted him as he entered the bar and one shouted an invitation to a game of chess. He refused.

'Coffee and cognac?' asked the waiter, Alberto, behind the bar. It wasn't really a question: Alvarez had had the same thing every evening after supper for as long as many could remember.

'How's life?' asked his neighbour, Torcuato, who worked in the small bottling plant nearby.

'I could complain, but no one would listen,' he replied.

Torcuato laughed. 'You're a miserable old bastard!'

'Can I help it if I was born unlucky?'

'Alberto!' shouted Torcuato to the waiter, 'pour Enrique a very large cognac to bring him back to life.'

'The whole bottle wouldn't do that,' replied the waiter.

'True enough — but it's worth trying.' Torcuato turned back to Alvarez. 'There's a good fight on telly tomorrow. You shouldn't miss it.'

'I'll try not to,' replied Alvarez, knowing full well he would not bother to watch the bull-fight.

'I saw your captain this morning, having a hell of a row with someone in the middle of the street. Thought there'd be murder done at any moment.'

'He's not my captain, thank God. My superior chief is way off, in Palma, where he can't bother me.'

'Lousy bastards, the guards, coming over from the Peninsula and throwing their weight about. As I said to the mayor, why the hell should we have to have all the guards from there so that they don't know a thing about the island or us islanders?'

'In order that you can't get pally enough to be stupid enough to try to bribe them to overlook your little hobby.'

There was loud laughter from those who'd been listening. Torcuato was known to be a successful smuggler in his spare time.

The waiter pushed across the bar a large black coffee and a very large cognac. 'Who's paying?'

'Him.' Alvarez pointed to Torcuato.

'By God!' exclaimed Torcuato, 'these policemen shake you down as bold as brass.' He slapped some coins on the counter.

'You call that a shake-down? You've got a lot to learn.'

Torcuato, never quite certain how to take Alvarez, beyond the fact that he was certainly incorruptible, muttered something he wras careful was not fully audible.

The waiter mopped the already clean bar, then stood in front of Alvarez and propped up his elbows. He looked as tired as he felt. 'Did you find the woman?'

'What woman?' Alvarez sipped the brandy.

'The Englishwoman who lives in José's place. You were looking for her this morning.'

Alvarez shook his head. 'No. She's not turned up.'

'They say she's come into a real fortune.'

Several men nearby stopped talking: money was a subject about which all of them were intensely interested.

'How's that?' asked Alvarez. 'Has she been along to tell you?'

There was brief laughter.

'She doesn't need to tell me anything. Andrés's wife works for the duchess.'

'So who's she?'

'That Englishwoman with a grand name and a face like she's a load of pig's shit right under it. What's she called exactly?' he asked everyone.

'She lives at Ca'n Lluxa,' said one man. But no one knew her name.

'Andrés's wife works for her,' continued the waiter. 'The old bag doesn't think the people she pays to work for her are human and have ears and she says anything in front of them ... D'you know, she doesn't let her husband into her bed!'

'Now try telling us about the mule that sings but won't talk,' said a large butcher.

'Straight. She doesn't let him in her bed because she can't stand it.'

'So why doesn't her husband clip her a smart one and teach her not to be such a stupid old bitch?'

No one could imagine why Lord Eastmore didn't act in such a reasonable manner, but several suggestions were made, none of them complimentary.

After a while, and when the suggestions had finally finished, Alvarez said: 'You were going to tell me about what Andrés's wife heard?'

The waiter removed his elbows from the counter and stood upright. 'Apparently this old woman who lives in José's house has come into a fortune from her godfather who's died in England. Millions and millions and millions of pesetas.'

'Sweet Jesus!' murmured someone reverently.

'If she's snuffed it,' said the waiter, 'it'll be an awful lot of money wasted, won't it?'

'You're ruining my evening by making me cry,' said Alvarez. 'Give me another large cognac, a Carlos this time and none of your cheap Fundador. My friend's still paying.'

'Damnation!' cried Torcuato. 'I haven't come into millions of pesetas. I'm just a poor honest workman.' He waited for the laughter to finish. 'If you're drinking on my pocket, Enrique, you're sticking to Fundador.'

'Stop fussing,' muttered the waiter. 'There's nothing but Fundador or Fabuloso in the place. People who come here can't afford anything better.'

*

'Charles,' said Lady Eastmore, as she stared at the giltwood mirror on her Louis XV dressing-table and applied to her cheeks the special rejuvenating cream she had flown out regularly from Monsieur Massoni of Bond Street, 'I had an interesting telephone call from Bertha earlier on.'

'Did you, dear?' Lord Eastmore was in his single bed and he was reading the previous day's issue of the *Financial Times*. Politicians, he noted, were talking about boom times ahead and this argued ill for the country's economy.

'She says that there's a very strong rumour that Elvina is missing.'

'Missing what, dear?'

'Charles, you have not been listening to me. You know very well how much I do dislike it when I talk to you, but you ignore every word I say.'

He laid the paper down on the bed.

'I said, Charles, that it appears likely Elvina Woods is missing.'

'Missing from where?'

'Where on earth is she likely to be missing from, except her house? Really, Charles, sometimes I think you set out deliberately to irritate me. That nephew of hers has called in the police … One would have thought that even a person like him would have had enough sense of responsibility not to do such a thing so soon — it could be so detrimental to the Community. I sincerely hope there's not going to be any sort of a scandal.'

'There usually is, when someone is missing. And if it concerns her, the scandal will be twice as bad, no doubt.' He picked up the newspaper and searched the share prices to see how ICI were doing.

*

Ignoring the tranquil beauty of the bay, almost ethereal because the air was still and the water mirror-flat, reflecting the moon in an unbroken shaft of luminosity, Mayans reached the shop as the bells of the church in the square struck midnight. He unlocked the door to the side of the shop entrance, shut it, and very carefully climbed the stairs.

Marie was in bed but not, as he had hoped, asleep. 'Where have you been?' she demanded.

'Don't shout,' he said. 'You'll wake up the old grandmother next door.'

'Wake her? When she died months ago ...? But you're drunk,' she said, in obvious surprise.

He stared stupidly at her. 'What did you think I was ...? Anyway, I'm not drunk.'

'I thought ...' She stopped. A wise wife did not say she thought he'd found himself a ripe, passionate woman. But a wise wife did remain on the attack. 'How dare you get drunk again, you filthy sot! You lied to me when you said you were only going out to ...'

'Shut up, just for a minute.'

'Don't you talk to me like that. I'm not going to be told to shut up in *my* house.'

'But I've some news.' He smiled at her, then sat down on the bed. She was wearing a nightdress and he ran his hand up her arm: she snatched it away. 'Good news. I heard it at the club.'

'So that's where you've been guzzling all my money.'

'Can't you ever calm down? They say that Señora Woods is missing.'

She relaxed back against the pillows and stared at him, wondering whether this was some drunken fantasy.

'Suppose she is dead? Eh? Suppose the old she-devil is dead?'

Marie remained silent.

'The lease is finished. It's over and done with.' He began to undress. His actions were all clumsy, but still under some control. 'We can get twelve or thirteen thousand a month. Maybe fourteen thousand.' He leaned forward. 'Get a stupid foreigner who says yes to everything and it could be as high as fifteen thousand.'

Her eyes were bright.

'So maybe I can sell that field to the Dutchman?'

She didn't say he couldn't.

He climbed into bed in his vest and long pants. He lay back and although the world went round for a while, it finally settled. He'd make half a million on the field. And the next letting of the house would line his pockets further. The ignorant peasants at the club weren't going to be able to laugh at him any longer.

*

Judy and Tatham were listening to the final ecstatic trio from *Der Rosenkavalier* when Ingham entered the music-room. He waved a quick good-evening at Tatham, sat down in one of the rather battered armchairs, and listened with them. The opera came to an end.

'When I need to reassure myself that I have a soul,' Ingham said, 'I play that record. Which I suppose is ironic, considering the earthiness of the story.'

'It's as if Strauss were for a while inspired beyond this world,' said Tatham.

'But to listen to some condescending critics, you'd think he was nothing but a third-rate composer who was lucky enough to produce a few catchy tunes. Who was it said: "Save me from my poor relations and all art critics"?'

'Some disgruntled old boor,' said Judy. 'Shaw, probably.'

'Sheer profanity, dear stepdaughter,' said Ingham lightly. He turned to Tatham. 'She refuses to recognize GBS possessed even the slightest ability on the good critical grounds that he was Irish, a Fabian, and a vegetarian.'

'You know very well it's because hardly any of his women could ever have really lived,' said Judy. Her tone of voice subtly changed. 'Larry, John's come with some rather disturbing news.'

'I'm sorry to hear that. What's the trouble? Can we help?'

Tatham said: 'Elvina's missing. She didn't return home last night after going out not long before dark to look for a plant. I'm afraid something must have happened to her.'

'Surely not? Knowing Elvina, I expect someone told her the flower she's chasing is up on the top of Puig Major and she's camped up there, trying to keep out of sight of the American army.'

'She was due to fly home this morning to get back to her godfather's funeral and she never turned up at the plane.'

'Oh! That does sound serious. I'm sorry I seemed to be treating it as a joke. What have you done?'

'I reported her disappearance to the police this morning, but although a detective came and saw me at the house, I've heard nothing since then. I came round here to see if you or Judy can suggest anything more I can do?'

'Have you any idea whereabouts this plant was supposed to be that she went looking for?'

'None at all. I don't even know from whom she heard about it. We went on a picnic lunch to Soller and stopped at Valldemossa on the way back. She couldn't be bothered to go round the monastery — said she'd done it much too often already and anyway it was nearly all pure fantasy about Chopin and Sand — so I left her at a café whilst I went round. I suppose she met someone there who told her. Anyway, when we got back she suddenly announced she was off and collected up her things. I tried to get her to leave the trip because she looked tired, but she wouldn't because she was off to London today ... And that's the last I saw of her. I've no idea, even, in which direction she set off.'

'But she left in her car?'

'Yes. And of course that's missing too, which is why I've had to hire one for a couple of days.'

'Then the police will find the car quickly enough. And ten to one, she'll have stayed at some hotel near where the flower is supposed to be. I like Elvina very much, John, but she does act very much on the spur of the moment.'

'When she's due to fly to London?'

'Yes, of course. I keep forgetting.' Ingham stood up. 'There's a quote which goes, roughly: "There's no catastrophe so great, not even a prolonged visitation from one's mother-in-law, which isn't lightened by a judicious dram." ... Judy, your usual? John, what would you like?'

'I think I'll have a gin and it, please.'

Ingham left the music-room.

Judy spoke in a comforting tone. 'I'm sure he's right, John. Elvina's just acted a little more casually than usual.' She hesitated. 'Even allowing for the flight.'

'I hope you're right,' he answered.

CHAPTER XV

THE GUARDIA CIVIL had the task of maintaining law and order in all rural areas of Spain and their Mobile Reserves patrolled the state highways. (Traffic duties in urban areas were carried out by the Policia Armada y de Trafico.) Most members of the Guardia Civil, since they were from the Peninsula, disliked the Mallorquins as much as the Mallor-quins disliked them, on grounds equally ridiculously xenophobic. They were an efficient, courteous body of men, provided people were courteous to them, and totally unbribable. It was two members of the Guardia Civil who sighted the Fiat 128 on Sunday morning.

The sun was rising beyond Cape Parelona and bathing the calm sea with fire as two members of the Mobile Reserve — like two jackdaws who signalled bad luck, said the locals, they never rode alone — drove up the road from Puerto Llueso in the direction of Parelona. With little possibility of other traffic — the waiters who worked at the Hotel Parelona would not be driving over the mountains for their early-morning shift just yet — the two motor-cyclists were enjoying using as much throttle as they dared, taking the acute corners at high speeds. When they reached the top, they turned into the parking area intending to have a short break before tackling the more hazardous down section to Parelona.

They saw the Fiat 128 shooting-brake with the red-banded number plates denoting tourist plates, remembered the order to look out for 1 PM 4325, and identified this as the car that was sought. One of them used his radio to call HQ.

The telephone in Alvarez's room, one of only two in the street, woke him. He yawned, saw the time was just after seven, remembered it was Sunday, and cursed. He lifted the receiver. 'Yeah?'

'Good morning. Good morning. It's a lovely day,' said the corporal.

'So that makes you happy. It makes me want to cut my throat.'

'I'm not stopping you … Listen, the Englishwoman's car has been found and I knew you'd want to hear immediately.'

'I couldn't sleep for waiting. Where is it?'

'In the car park by the viewing point on the road to Parelona. D'you know it?'

'Never heard of it. Never been near it. Wouldn't know it if I saw it.'

'Great. You'll have a gay bundle looking for it.'

The line went dead. Why, thought Alvarez bleakly, did things like this always happen on a Sunday? He ran his tongue round his mouth and wondered what in the name of Satan it tasted like — a possible answer didn't make him feel any healthier. His head thumped. He'd drunk a hell of a lot of brandy the previous night. He shut his eyes. Couldn't the bloody car wait? What if twenty Englishwomen went missing? Good riddance to the lot of'em.

If her car was up there on the mountain, he thought as he lay back, it was only reasonable to suppose that she was dead. No other explanation seemed possible. She'd gone to search for some flowers — queer that an Englishwoman should be bothered to enjoy the countryside sufficiently to search it for flowers she didn't always pick, but just identified — and had taken a tumble over the edge. Up there, nothing was simpler than falling.

He opened his eyes again, groaned, sat up, groaned again, then finally climbed out of bed. He put on trousers and went along to the bathroom. Downstairs, he took from the refrigerator a bowl of soup and warmed a cupful into which he crumbled a couple of slices of pan Mallorquin. The soup finished, he had a brandy, then, feeling slightly more healthy, he went out to his rusting Seat parked in the street. Several children were playing in the road. He looked briefly at them and thought with real pleasure how well fed they obviously were: he could remember thin faces, paunchy bellies, rickets, kids without the energy to play at anything much.

The drive up to the viewing point in the mountains took him half an hour; the Seat 600 laboured up the steeper sections of road and almost came to a stop at the tightest right-hander. He turned into the car park and drew up alongside the Fiat. When he climbed out of his car, he stared out to sea. It was glassy and the heat had not yet built up enough to confuse the horizon so there was a sharply etched line between the two blues of sea and sky. A fishing-boat chugged slowly along, leaving behind a short wake. It was a beautiful place in which to die, he decided.

He opened the passenger door of the Fiat. On the seat were some plastic boxes, a book, a battered handbag, a camera in a case, and a torch — it was a wonder no thieving tourist had stolen some of the items. The book was open at a page which detailed plants peculiar to Mallorca. *Scutellaria balearica*, in the text, was underlined and there was a question mark in the margin. He'd never heard of it. Presumably that was the plant she'd been seeking. He replaced the book on the seat, opened the handbag and shuffled through the contents. There was the flight ticket and the telegram. He went round to the back of the car and lifted up the tailgate. On the black flooring was a four-centimetre length of rough woollen thread, coloured a bright yellow, reddish circles from the base of butano bottles, and nothing else. He carried on round and sat down in the driving seat. Great to be a foreigner, raping the country with money, buying a car like this and not having to pay the luxury tax on it. Some difference from his Seat 600. He took a driving position and found the seat was too far back for him to be able to work the pedals with any degree of assurance. This caused him to notice that he could also not gain a reasonable view in the rear-view mirror. Elderly Englishwomen came two metres tall, thin, juiceless.

He left the Fiat and walked to the edge of the cliff, looked down, seemed to sway, and very hastily stepped back. He'd no head for heights and a drop like this one made him mentally collapse.

If the señora had been searching here for that plant she could have fallen at any point and the fall might or might not leave traces. There were bare patches of rock, pockets of shallow earth, clumps of spiny grass, dwarf fan palms (once used for making poufs), prickly ground creeper, and the debris of the thousands of tourists who'd visited the place. He didn't expect to find any trace of a fall, yet to the left he came across a scraping mark through a pocket of earth and a smear of black (from a shoe?) on rock. Taking his life in his hands, or stomach, he lay down and looked over the edge. There was an outcrop of rock not far below and then the stomach-churning drop down to the sea.

He returned to his Seat, sat down behind the wheel, and lit a cigarette. There really wasn't anything more to be done. She'd fallen over the edge while looking for a plant. Maybe her body would be washed up, maybe it wouldn't. The Englishman had better come and collect the car, else some foreigner would pinch it. He removed the camera, book, handbag, and torch, locked up, and pocketed the key. He drove back down to the Puerto and Llueso.

*

Judy manoeuvred the Seat as close to the Fiat as she could get. 'I hope it isn't too awful for you?' she asked, in her most direct manner, yet with unmistakable concern.

Roderic Jeffries

He looked at her and wondered how she could have the capacity to be both so considerate and yet so contemptuously indifferent towards others. 'No, it isn't. I liked Elvina a lot, but there isn't the bitter sorrow there would be if she'd been a close relative or I'd known her for years. Can you understand what I mean?'

'Sincere regrets, but no tears.'

'That's about it. If she did fall down somewhere here, it must surely have been quick. You can't wish anyone much better than that.'

'I suppose not. I do hope they ... they find her. I'm being stupid, but I hate to think of her body never being found.'

'Would it worry you, then, what happened to your body after you're dead?'

'That's one of those unanswerable questions. If I have a soul, that's all I need to worry about; if I haven't, I won't have the capacity to be worried afterwards.'

He opened his door and climbed out. He leaned down to say to her: 'I'll drive straight back to your house and we'll go out to lunch at that place on the Creyola road you mentioned, shall we?'

'That would be great.'

He left and went round half-a-dozen parked cars to the Fiat, unlocked it, and sat behind the wheel. As always, the engine was reluctant to start, but he finally got it to fire by pressing the accelerator on the floor. He blipped the throttle several times until the engine was responding cleanly, moved in the choke, engaged reverse, and backed out past the mobile ice-cream van which was doing a good trade because a coach had recently drawn into the car park and unloaded its passengers.

Unless Elvina's body was soon discovered, he thought as he began the downhill drive, application would have to be made to the courts to presume her dead, as it would in England. Did one have to wait long before such presumption became absolute? In any case, he must leave the island before too long because his money wasn't endless. And how long before he discovered whether Geoffrey Maitland had willed the bulk of his fortune to Elvina and Elvina had altered her will with all due care and formality proper to someone living in Spain?

*

The Hevia brothers lived in Cala Paraitx, in two small houses at the back of the hotel. Both in their late sixties, the elder was married, the younger not. All their working lives they had been fishermen. They could remember, as they'd tell anyone who'd listen, when Cala Paraitx, one of the scenic wonders of the island, had been inaccessible except by boat or fifteen-kilometre-long mule track, so that few people came to visit it. They could remember that twice torrential rain had persisted for so long the torrente, which normally flowed gently along the canyon which ran between gaunt brooding mountains inland to Creyola, had boiled with water to the extent that each time they had really believed the second Flood was under way. They could also remember when the sea was so full of fish that their catch was always heavy, but now pollution and over-fishing had reduced their catches to the point where it sometimes seemed hardly worth while taking the few fish along to the hotel and there was nothing to send over the mountains to Creyola.

They boarded their boat, made in Puerto Llueso fifteen years before, at six-fifteen, Tuesday morning. Mario, the elder of the two and the mechanic, started the engine after fifteen minutes of hard swearing. Victor cast off and steered them out of the cove, with cliffs swooping down into the sea, automatically going to starboard of the patch of darker blue which marked a fang of rock that rose within half a metre of the surface.

They were using long lines, each with more than a hundred hooks that were baited with squid. When these were laid and buoyed, they stopped the engine and floated a kilometre off the rocky, dangerous coast, moving gently to the slight swell. They drank wine, ate thick slabs of bread with oil and salt on them, and talked about the past in the simplest of terms.

Victor saw the body: his eyesight had always been the keener of the two. He was watching a black-headed gull and wondering whether it might be over a shoal of fish when he saw floating under it a bundle of something. He pointed it out to Mario who swore there was nothing there, but who was finally persuaded to restart the engine.

When they found it was a badly battered body they were annoyed that it was nothing salvageable, but, being primitive philosophers, they shrugged their shoulders and returned to their yarning and their fishing. Later, they landed a better catch of fish than they had had for some time, so — almost in a spirit of thanks to the fates — Victor trudged along to the hotel and told the cook, an old friend of theirs, to telephone the Guardia Civil at Creyola.

*

The body was brought ashore at Cala Paraitx just before dark. A small crowd of tourists — ghoulish bastards, thought Alvarez — gathered round and watched.

Alvarez stared down at the sodden body. Dark blue woollen dress, woollen tights, thick black walking shoes ... The old girl must have suffered from bad blood circulation. She was dressed for the winter, yet since Friday it had been warm, almost hot.

'Is it all right to get moving?' asked the driver of the small open van which had been hired to take the body over the mountains.

'Yeah. And when you get to the morgue tell 'em I'll be on to the next-of-kin to arrange with undertakers immediately.'

'Sure.'

The law said a body must be buried within twenty-four hours of death — very necessary in high summer. A doctor must examine this body to conform with regulations, but as soon as that was done the funeral must be fixed up at once. Where did non-Catholics get planted? At the back of his mind was the memory of reading that there was a small cemetery in Palma for foreigners of bogus faiths.

He helped the driver load the body-wrapped up in canvas and infuriatingly difficult to handle — on to the back of the van. The driver, who'd climbed up, pulled the canvas towards the cab and by heaving it diagonally it was just possible to fit it in. 'It's a good job she wasn't a large 'un,' said the driver, 'or we'd have had to leave her feet sticking up.'

She *was* small, though Alvarez: small enough to have been a Mallorquin. But that was odd ... He saw the driver was just about to jump down. 'Hang on up there for a moment.'

'What the hell for?'

'Because I tell you to.'

'That's great, but I'm in a hurry. It's no fun driving this thing over the mountains in the dark.' But the driver stayed where he was because only a fool got too far on the wrong side of the police.

'How tall was she?' asked Alvarez.

'How the hell would I know?' replied the driver sullenly.

'Try guessing.'

The driver unwrapped the canvas and stared at the body. 'One metre sixty, sixty-five maybe.'

In other words, thought Alvarez, within a couple of centimetres of his own height. Yet when he'd sat in the Fiat up in the mountains he'd found that the seat was too far back for him to work the pedals or look into the rear-view mirror.

'Can I start?' demanded the driver.

'Get moving, but see she gets there safely.' Alvarez dropped his cigarette stub on to the floor and stamped it out, then lit another. He stared at the onlookers without actually seeing them, and tried to assure himself that a mad Englishwoman might easily set the driving seat of her car so far back she couldn't drive safely. But he couldn't really accept the proposition. And someone at the club in Llueso had said she'd come into a packet of money ... Forget it, he told himself. Ten to one the position of the driving seat didn't mean a thing. If he settled for the obvious, there'd be one or two forms to fill in and then that would be that. But start asking questions and God knows where things would end. And it wasn't as if it were important — no Spaniard or Mallorquin was involved.

As the van left, he returned to his car, a borrowed Seat 127-his Seat 600 would never have made the journey — and not very different from a Fiat 128. He slid the driving seat right back and this left his feet only just able to make contact with the pedals. He switched on the engine, engaged first gear, and released the clutch. His left foot slipped and the car went into a series of kangaroo hops which only ended when the engine stalled. A hippie-type couple in their early twenties laughed at him. Unwashed English, he thought furiously, since he prided himself on his ability as a driver.

CHAPTER XVI

TATHAM WAS READING through the previous day's *Daily Telegraph*, bought that morning from the newsagent down in the Puerto, when he heard a car come up the dirt-track. He looked out through the window of the dining recess and saw a white Seat 600, and although there was nothing at that stage to give him a definite identification he was fairly certain it was the detective's car.

He folded up the newspaper, went through to the hall, and opened the front door. The Seat didn't stop until the bonnet was under the balcony. Alvarez climbed out.

Alvarez looked more crumpled and used-up than before, thought Tatham. Yet there was a suggestion in the lines about his heavy mouth which said he was a man who could quickly smarten up if ever he wanted to.

'Good afternoon, Señor Tatham. I hope I find you well?' He said he was fine as he relaxed slightly. This must be a formal visit or the detective could surely never be so courteous?

'I fear I have some bad news for you, Señor. We have recovered a body which we believe to be the señora's.'

Tatham fidgeted with the button of his shirt, trying to give the impression of a man who was suddenly faced with an event which he had been expecting yet had been hoping against hope would not arise. 'I see.' He even managed to speak hoarsely.

'I have to ask you to come to identify the body.'

'Must I?' The revulsion in his voice was genuine.

Alvarez nodded. 'And as you will be identifying her, Señor, I must have certain details for the records. May we go somewhere where I can write?'

He led the way inside into the dining recess where the table offered the best writing surface. 'Would you like some coffee?' he asked.

'Nothing for me, thank you. But if I may see your passport, please, and do you have the name and address of the señora's lawyers?'

'You want the address of her lawyers?'

'She has personal property here, a bank account no doubt, and the law has to know what to do with it all. In these unfortunate cases, we always have a word with the deceased's legal advisers.'

'Yes, of course. I just wasn't thinking.' He left, realizing how a perfectly ordinary request had nearly sent him into a mental flat spin. He had, he told himself, to be more careful. Because he knew the truth, he was suspecting hidden meanings where there weren't any.

His passport was in the inside breast pocket of his coat which hung in the cupboard of his bedroom. He went into the solar and across to the desk and searched through the drawers, finding Elvina's address book: under 'Solicitors' was the name of a firm in Rockton Cross.

Downstairs, Alvarez put on his heavy horn-rimmed glasses and noted down the address and name of the firm. He handed the address book back and examined the passport, looked up after a short while. 'This says you are a farmer?'

'That's right. I am.'

'How many hundreds of hectares do you farm?' he asked, and could not keep the hostility from his voice.

'None at all, right now,' replied Tatham, puzzled by the other's attitude.

'But many hundreds before you sold and came out to this island?'

'I rented seventy acres at an uneconomic rent. I had forty-five cows and sometimes couldn't even get enough grass off the seventy acres to keep them in milk. The soil was thick yellow clay and the only time that's any good is in a drought which doesn't last too long, when the grass will keep growing where it dries up on lighter soils ...' He stopped, then said: 'I'm sorry. Ask me one question on farming and I'm off.'

'Off where?'

'Off talking about it, twenty to the dozen.'

'You sounded very enthusiastic?'

'Well, of course. Wouldn't you expect that?'

'My parents were on the land,' said Alvarez. Strange, for a moment the Englishman had sounded just like a peasant farmer who understood the feel of soil trickling through his fingers. A pose? He looked back at the passport. 'I shall have to keep this for a short time. I do not suppose you are intending to return immediately to England?'

'No, I'm not. There'll be the funeral to arrange and probably several other things to cope with.'

'Exactly. So I will take the passport and issue you a receipt for it. Should you need to leave the country unexpectedly, come to the station of the Guardia Civil in the village and ask for me.' He wrote out a receipt, on a form ready stamped with the police seal, and handed this across. 'Now, we unfortunately have the identification. Shall we proceed in your car?'

'If you like,' replied Tatham, wondering why this should be more convenient than each using his own car.

When they sat down in the Fiat, Alvarez noticed that the driving seat was considerably farther back than the passenger seat: a setting which obviously suited this long-legged Englishman. Judging visually, it was the same setting at which it had been when the car had been found up in the mountains.

They drove down the dirt-track, turned the corner and were slowly passing the fields on their right, occasional loose stones clunking on the underneath of the car, when Tatham stopped. 'You can tell me something since you'll know about the land. I've asked and no one else knows the answer.' He pointed to the land on his right where crops were being grown underneath orange and lemon trees. 'Why are there so many different clumps of the same crop? Three separate lots of tomatoes, artichokes there and there, chick peas going slantwise, one group of lettuces in a circle, another right over there, beans here and beans there. Why not put all the plants of one variety together? Wouldn't that surely make for much easier cultivation?'

'You think, probably, the peasant is a fool? He's never had the intelligence to think of anything so advanced?'

'On the contrary,' retorted Tatham, annoyed by the other's surliness. 'It's because no good farmer is a fool that I wonder why this chap doesn't make things easier for himself — judging by the look of his crops, he's a very good market-gardener.'

Alvarez lit a cigarette. 'I don't know why,' he finally muttered.

Tatham didn't believe him. He engaged first gear and drove on, stopping where the dirt-track met the road to let a car pass. 'Which end of the town do we need to go to?' 'At the far end, so start along the Palma road.' Alvarez relapsed into silence and smoked quickly, only speaking again to direct Tatham through the narrow streets of Llueso to the morgue. There were two rooms on the ground floor at the back of an undertaker's: in one room were three wooden chairs, in the other a marble slab. Tatham was left in the first room for a few minutes, during which he smoked and stared at the damp stains at the base of the walls, then he was called into the second room. He took a deep breath, swallowed nervously, stood up, and went in. The reality was not as bad as imagination had suggested and he was in control of himself when he said: 'Yes. She's my great-aunt, Elvina Woods.'

The white sheet was drawn back over the body by the grim-faced man who was the town's undertaker. Alvarez motioned Tatham to follow him out and back to the first room. 'We can return to your house, now.'

'Can you tell me what happens next?'

'There are certain formalities to be followed.'

'But what do I do about the funeral?'

'I will tell you as soon as you should start arrangements. Then you may speak to the man we have just met. He is the only undertaker in Llueso.'

They returned to the Fiat and drove back towards Ca'n Manin and as they rattled along the dirt-track, past the field with the many patches of crops which had puzzled Tatham, Alvarez said, without any preamble and as if the question had just been put to him: 'It is perhaps a question of water. Here, on this island, we have weeks and months without rain and crops have to be irrigated very often. The farmers are not rich and cannot afford automatic irrigation, so they cut channels through the soil and run water down the channels. The land is terraced, but each field does not always slope exactly and some parts can be well watered and some cannot. But as you know, each crop needs a different degree of water.' The moment he'd spoken, he was annoyed he'd done so. Yet he wasn't going to have this Englishman think him such a fool that he knew nothing about farming.

'Of course!' said Tatham. 'I ought to have realized that.' He tried to speak lightly. 'But at home our problem in the summer is usually too much rain, not too little. Have you ever been to England?'

'No,' muttered Alvarez, and he made even that one word bad-tempered.

Like a politician, thought Tatham: changing attitudes almost as fast as he breathed.

When they reached Ca'n Manin, Alvarez refused a drink, said goodbye with curt briefness, and left. Tatham checked on the time, then returned to the car and drove the kilometre to Ca'n Xema. Judy was in. She greeted him with obvious pleasure.

'They've found Elvina,' he said abruptly.

'Oh!' She ran her hands through her long black hair and looked at him.

'Her body was in the sea, somewhere near Cala Paraitx. I've just been along to a place in Llueso to identify her.'

'How perfectly beastly for you. Come through and have a really stiff drink to help.' She tucked her arm round his. 'Shall we play some music to take you out of yourself or would you rather talk about it?'

'I'll settle for the music afterwards, but first off I must have your advice on what I've got to do, because the detective wasn't very helpful.'

She led the way into the music-room and as he sat down she crossed to the glass-fronted cupboard in which a large number of records were stored in racks. 'The funeral has to be held very quickly by law. Especially in this case, because …' She didn't finish.

'He did tell me he'd let me know when I could speak to the undertaker.'

She showed her surprise. 'Let you know? But didn't he want you to make all arrangements immediately?'

'No. Is that so very odd?'

She nibbled her lower lip for a few seconds. 'Maybe after an accident like this it's different …'

She looked at him with obvious perplexity and he realized that there was far more significance in what had happened than he had imagined. For the first time, he disturbingly began to realize that things weren't going as smoothly as he had believed.

*

Death was the great democrat. Everybody died, even the Eastmores of the world, so everybody acknowledged it and there was no disgrace in dying. General respect was paid to everyone, even those who in their lifetime had been outside the Community and irrespective of how serious their past social solecisms.

'Charles,' said Lady Eastmore, as she sipped her cognac — Cognac, not Spanish brandy — 'I hear that Elvina's body has been found. It was in the sea.'

'That means the funeral tomorrow.' Lord Eastmore frowned. 'I hope I have a black tie?'

'Two new ones which I bought at Crampton's for you. It's all rather inconvenient, as a matter of fact: Norah and I were going into Palma tomorrow.'

The mountain was eating her way through a large plateful of French crystallized fruit. 'Who's the man we met at drinks who told me, Mary?'

'Reggie. A reasonable man when he's not tight.'

119

The mountain hesitated between a plum and half an apricot. She chose the apricot, popped it into her mouth, licked the traces of sugar off her thumb and forefinger, and began to chew. 'He said he reckoned there was something very odd going on.'

'What did he mean?' asked Lady Eastmore, with interest.

'It's something to do with not allowing the funeral to take place yet.' She swallowed, noisily cleared her teeth with her tongue, picked up the plum, and resumed chewing.

'Charles,' said Lady Eastmore, 'isn't that all very odd? The authorities usually insist on the funeral almost before the person's properly dead.'

'Quite so,' he answered.

'Trust Elvina to make an unfortunate spectacle even out of her own funeral!'

*

Mayans ran up the stairs to their flat. It was immediately obvious Marie was in the sitting-room and he went in there. She was at the table, counting money and checking figures with the help of a manually operated adding-machine.

'They've found her,' he said breathlessly.

Her hand was on the handle of the adding-machine and she automatically operated it before saying: 'D'you mean Señora Woods?'

'Floating off Paraitx and couldn't be deader. Marie, the house is ours.'

'It's mine,' she corrected sharply. She looked at him, then began to stack up the money.

He crossed to the old Mallorquin sideboard he'd bought in the Palma flea market and picked up from it a two-and-a-half-litre bottle of 501 brandy. 'Fifteen thousand a month, now the old bitch has popped it.' He suddenly crossed himself. 'And that crazy Dutchman will pay two and a ...' He stopped, aghast at what he'd been about to say. 'Two million pesetas for the field.'

She finished stacking the money and with a sigh of relief Mayans realized she hadn't divined what he'd almost said.

CHAPTER XVII

IT WAS ALWAYS a lottery as to whether a telephone call to Palma went through as clear as a bell or was strangled by interference so that barely every other word was audible. On Wednesday morning, it was perfectly clear.

'Why do you recommend a post-mortem?' asked Superior Chief Salas.

Alvarez leaned back in his chair and rested his feet on the desk. He sighed. 'As I've just explained …'

Salas was not a man to allow anyone to explain anything unchecked. 'You say this woman fell down the cliff at the viewing site on the Llueso/Parelona road? Don't you find that good enough reason for death?'

'I just want to check …'

'Have you the slightest idea what a post-mortem costs?'

'I know they're expensive …'

'Who is she? Only a foreigner.'

'I know, Senor, but …'

'If I go to the Institute of Forensic Anatomy and ask Professor Romero to conduct a post-mortem, I receive a bill for thousands of pesetas. No doubt you are unconcerned about spending pesetas, but I have to worry …'

Alvarez stared gloomily through the window. Sharp sunshine speared down into the narrow street and people were beginning to walk on the shady side. He was a fool. Even after all these years, he had not learned an ounce of common sense. All he'd had to do was get the doctor to agree the woman's injuries were consistent with falling down the cliff face into the sea — and who was going to disagree with that? — and the case would have been all wrapped up. But he'd had to get clever. Like a man approaching his dotage, he'd …

'Do you still insist on a post-mortem?' demanded Superior Chief Salas.

'It's not for me to insist, Señor, but I must recommend it. There are a few odd points to clear up.'

'Odd points! Cleared up! As if the whole matter were simply a case of a handful of pesetas which would not disturb my department's budget …! Very well,' he grumbled. 'Arrange to have the body driven to Palma immediately, together with all the necessary documents. And is it also *your* request for forwarding to Interpol that has come through from Llueso?'

'Yes, Senor.'

'You seem to be conducting a one-man crusade against crime.' He slammed down the receiver.

Alvarez's thoughts became still gloomier. He'd reminded his superiors that he existed. If he went even farther and uncovered and solved a murder, he might, God knows, even at this late stage be given promotion and be moved from Llueso. The thought so distressed him that he bent down and opened the bottom drawer of the desk, brought out a litre bottle of Fundador, and poured himself out a large drink.

The telephone rang and after a while he lifted the receiver. Palma said that a report had just been received from England, via Interpol. Señora Woods had very recently made a fresh will which left her estate — except for a few minor bequests — to her great-nephew, John Alexander Tatham. Her lawyers reported that her estate had been small prior to the death of Señor Maitland, her godfather, who had predeceased her by a very short time, the preceding Thursday in fact, but he had willed his estate to her and although the full extent of this would not be known for months, it could not be less than one million pounds sterling.

He thanked his informant, replaced the receiver, picked up a pencil and wrote down a million. He looked through the day's newspaper for the current rate of exchange for a pound sterling and found it was around one hundred and thirty-five. A hundred and thirty-five million, he wrote — not realizing that in a democratic country one was democratically forced to pay immense death duties in a proportion beyond the belief of a Spaniard, beyond the comprehension of a Mallorquin. One hundred and thirty-five million. For that sum of money, many men would murder not only a great-aunt but also all their aunts, cousins, sisters, brothers, mother and father as well.

Señor Maitland had died on Thursday, Señora Woods on Friday night. Rushing it a bit. Wouldn't a murderer have waited so that the two deaths combined did not have such an obvious significance? But maybe there had been rows and Señora Woods had threatened to change her will. Or Tatham had been so greedy he couldn't wait? Or he thought his faked accident could never be uncovered? Or he thought the police wouldn't be interested in what a foreigner got up to? Or he hadn't thought?

He brought out a packet of cigars from his pocket and lit one. After arranging for the body to be driven to the Institute in Palma, he must find out whether a maid wras employed at Ca'n Manin and, if so, have a talk with her.

He'd also like a look round the house, another check on the flower book …

Sweet Jesus, he thought, life could become so rushed that a man no longer had time to live.

*

Tatham was sitting out on the patio under the vine, some of whose shoots were now over two metres long, when the Seat 600 came round the corner. The detective again. To tell him that at long last the burial could go ahead? He lifted his glass and drained it and quite suddenly his hand was shaking and he recognized the extent to which tension had been building up within himself.

'Good morning, Señor,' said Alvarez. His clothes looked a little less crumpled, as if he'd taken just a little care over his appearance.

Tatham offered a drink and this was accepted with alacrity. He went through to the larder and poured out a very large brandy and a sweet Cinzano for himself, returned to the patio and sat down opposite the other. Almost at once, their conversation concerned farming in England and soon he was detailing all the things he would have done had he had the money.

'Money always seems to be the problem,' said Alvarez.

'It certainly is in farming today. You can't live off a small-holding and that means a minimum of a hundred acres to be economic, which calls for something over a hundred and fifty thousand pounds. Then, you won't get the return on capital you would elsewhere.'

'So if you had a great deal of money, you would not return to a farm?'

Tatham shook his head. 'I'd be illogical enough to return to farming as quickly as possible. I'd aim for a hundred and fifty acres …' Once again he detailed his plans.

'All this modern machinery you talk about is very expensive?'

'Yes. But with us labour's more expensive in the long run and far less reliable.'

'It is happening even here. Look at that orange grove.' Alvarez pointed. 'No crops are being grown under the trees: only weeds. Yet thirty years ago the ground would have been filled. This area is called La Huerta de Llueso. That means it is the market-garden of Llueso. But fewer and fewer crops are grown here even though the soil is rich. The farmers want more money than they can earn by traditional methods, so they move to other tasks.'

'And the mule carts will disappear, there'll be no donkeys kicking up a racket, no hobbled sheep or hobbled chickens gleaning, and men will have lost all contact with the only thing that really matters, the soil. It's a tragedy.'

'A tragedy,' agreed Alvarez. Then he suffered a sharp astonishment. Here was he, agreeing with, and even apparently in sympathy with, an Englishman! An Englishman, moreover, who had probably murdered his own great-aunt. He spoke quickly. 'I fear I must stop talking, Señor, and return to work.' He lifted his glass and drained it. 'But before I leave, would it be too disturbing to show me inside the finca? I've always had an interest in old farmhouses and this one seems unusually large. But perhaps that's because the cattle shed at the end has been drawn into the building?' Tatham showed him around the house and was interested to be told what the place had probably been like before it was altered and modernized. He failed to notice the interest Alvarez took in the many-coloured, rough-woven bedspreads.

As they returned outside, Alvarez said: 'You must need a maid with a place this size?'

'My aunt had one who came every afternoon. Catalina's wonderful: she copes with everything.'

'She lives nearby, if she comes in the afternoons?'

'Very close. Just two roads away from the Roman bridge. Her husband works for a master builder and she's two young kids who need a lot of feeding, so she's very glad to get the extra money.'

'I'm told that one of the things the foreigners like about this country is that they can hire maids cheaply. Of course, soon there will be no cheap maids, just as there will be no peasant farmers.'

Tatham caught the bitterness in the detective's voice and looked across, but the other's face was almost expressionless.

'By the way,' said Alvarez, 'I need to know the name of the plant Señora Woods was searching for?'

'What on earth for?'

Alvarez shrugged his shoulders. 'You can have no idea how the minds of the officials work. The least detail becomes of the utmost significance. It would, perhaps, be best if you lend me the book that was in the señora's car on the night when she so unfortunately died and I can copy out everything that's needed.'

Tatham went into the house and picked up the book from the long shelf in the hall. He brought it out.

'Thank you very much. It is obviously an expensive book and I will look after it well.'

Alvarez shook hands before climbing into his Seat. He drove off, noisily because the car squeaked badly as it lurched into potholes on the dirt-track. Tatham watched it until it disappeared round the corner. It had on the surface been a pleasant meeting, with the detective at one stage offering a sympathy of understanding he had not done before … But there'd been no permission to arrange the funeral and not even any reason given for the visit. Tatham felt more afraid than he had been.

*

The two men from Essen, one tall and thin, one short and fat, so that Ingham thought of them as Laurel and Hardy, were very formal. 'Thank you, Herr Ingham,' they said in unison. The tall and thin one added: 'We have seen everything we wish.'

'And have you found any impending catastrophes, such as a collapsing roof?' asked Ingham.

There were no smiles. 'Naturally, Herr Ingham, you cannot expect me … us … to give you any details of our survey, which are for Herr Naupert's eyes alone, but I can venture so far as to say that your house is generally in excellent order. A charming gentleman's residence. May I congratulate you on the taste with which it has been built.'

'Very kind of you,' murmured Ingham.

The tall thin man stepped forward, briefcase under his left arm, stretched out his right arm, and shook hands. The short fat man followed suit.

Ingham watched them drive off, then returned into the hall. 'Judy,' he called out. 'Come on down and have a drink. They've gone.'

He watched her descend the curving staircase, one hand on the elegant wrought-iron banisters he had patterned on some he'd seen in a manor house in Seville. She was — when she wasn't sulking — very attractive, he thought, mainly — and if this wasn't becoming too Irish — because she was not particularly beautiful: her attraction was one of intelligent character, not physical perfection. Which was odd, because her mother was very beautiful and quite unintelligent.

When she reached the floor, she said: 'Who was the mysterious second man, the fat one, who didn't know what to do?'

She'd picked out the fraud immediately, even after the briefest of introductions. Just occasionally, he thought, she was too intelligent.

She studied his face, her dark brown eyes intent, then she crossed the hall, her heels clacking slightly on the beautiful hand-painted tiles, and went into the sitting-room. She stood in front of the Renoir and when he followed her in, she said: 'Larry, I don't know what's happening, but does it have to?'

'Nothing's happening,' he answered.

'Don't keep treating me like a fool.' Her voice was sharp. 'I know things are very tight, financially. And that's why you've gone all out to persuade Naupert to buy this house at more than it's worth. But he's a hard businessman who, to judge by the only time I've seen him, has never paid more than it's worth for anything. So how have you tempted him?'

He was about to start another total denial of her implied accusation when he realized that that would be stupid. Instead, he said: 'If he buys this house, I'll have done nothing illegal. The most I'll have done is dangle a piece of bait in front of him which a truly honest man wouldn't take. He'll be able to blame no one but himself if he snaps hard and finds himself hooked and landed.'

'Would a truly honest man dangle the bait in the first instance?'

'What was the name of the angel who promised to make a saint of the first truly honest man he met, but returned to Heaven wiser, tired, and with the halo still in his hand?'

'You so often refuse to answer a question directly, don't you? Larry, I'm worried. I don't want to see you in the most terrible trouble.'

He smiled, his face creasing so that the lines of dissolution momentarily became lines of good humour. 'People like me never really land in trouble. We always manage just to skirt it.'

*

'Mary,' said Mrs Cabbott, 'you keep the best table I've ever known. And that wine! It was like liquid velvet.'

Lady Eastmore pressed the bell-push under the table to summon the butler and the maid.

'Freddie, wasn't that just the most delicious wine you've ever drunk?' asked Mrs Cabbott.

'Not a bad bit of plonk,' answered Cabbott. 'Speaking for myself, though, I prefer a good jorum of foaming ale. Wine for the gentlemen, beer for the officers, what!'

'Freddie,' said Mrs Cabbott furiously, 'stop blathering. You know perfectly well you simply adore a superb wine like the one we've just had.'

He guffawed. 'Put my big foot in it, have I? Reminds me of old Colonel Sparrow. More like a bloody great vulture, he was. "Wine," he'd shout, when the mess waiter tried to pour him some, "that stuff's only fit for women and the effete aristocracy" …'

'Oh, God!' moaned Mrs Cabbott.

Miguel and the maid came into the room and Fru-Fru trotted in after them. The maid cleared the dirty plates and glasses, watched morosely by Miguel who lusted after her, but was making no progress.

'Do you prefer cheese before or after the dessert?' asked Lady Eastmore, as she fed Fru-Fru a morsel of meat she'd saved on her side plate.

'Whichever you like,' replied Mrs Cabbott. 'I'm very easy.'

'As the actress remarked to the bishop as she slipped off her stays,' said her husband.

Mrs Cabbott closed her eyes.

'Cheese afterwards,' pronounced Lady Eastmore.

Cabbott turned to Lord Eastmore. 'Remember me telling you about that imshi from the Bank of England who was chasing out dirty money? Got old Morley in his obscene clutches?'

'I vaguely remember something,' replied Lord Eastmore.

'Well the news is good now. He's buggered off the island.'

'Freddie!' shrieked his wife.

Miguel, recognizing one of the few words he knew in English, looked down his nose.

'He's gone back to England, and that's what I said, isn't it? No one's told him any more tales, I suppose, so he has to call the rest of us honest. Does that make you feel more cheerful, Charles?'

Lord Eastmore smiled briefly.

*

Mayans arrived at Ca'n Manin with his brother-in-law, a pleasant, middle-aged, round-faced, soft-spoken man with five front gold teeth which gave him a sparkling smile.

'My brother-in-law,' said the brother-in-law, 'wishes to express his deep sorrow at the death of the senõra.'

No one, thought Tatham, had ever looked less sorrowful. 'That's very kind of him. Won't you both sit down?'

The brother-in-law spoke in Mallorquin to Mayans and they sat down. Mayans looked around the sitting-room with a proprietary stare.

'My brother-in-law wishes to say he is very sorry to have to say what he has come to say.'

Tatham put off the sad moment for a while and offered them a drink and they both chose brandy. He poured them out large drinks, but had nothing himself.

'My brother-in-law has to say that the lease of this house is now at an end. He wishes to know what you will be doing and the rent will be fifteen thousand pesetas a month.'

'How did my aunt pay the rent?' asked Tatham. There was a short conference. 'The señora paid each month, on the tenth.'

'Then there are still several days to go on the present month's rent before the lease expires.'

'My brother-in-law says no, the lease ended when she died. If you wish to stay in this house ...'

'I'm certainly staying until I've arranged the funeral and cleared up my aunt's estate.'

There was a much longer conference, during which the pitch of Mayans's voice rose considerably.

'My brother-in-law is pleased if you stay, but it will be necessary to pay a bigger rent.'

'If the rent is paid until the tenth of next month, I'm surely entitled to stay here until then without paying anything even though my aunt has died? If there's going to be an argument, though, we'd better have it through lawyers.' Another consultation. 'My brother-in-law says that lawyers are very expensive in this country.'

'They usually are in any country.'

'Perhaps it would be best if you stay here until the tenth. But after that, the rent is fifteen thousand. My brother-in-law is sorry, but property is expensive today.'

'Very expensive,' agreed Tatham drily.

They finished their drinks and stood up. The brother-in-law half bowed, then shook hands as he flashed his golden teeth. 'It is a very good pleasure to meet you.'

Mayans expressed no such sentiment.

CHAPTER XVIII

ALVAREZ STEPPED inside the opened doorway of the house, which brought him into the impeccably clean and tidy sitting-room, and called out: 'Señora Calbo?'

An old woman, face wrinkled like a prune, dressed in black, came through from the kitchen, which lay beyond the sitting-room.

'Is Señora Calbo in?' he asked. 'I'm from the Cuerpo General de Policia.'

Her expression became frightened and she turned and hurried up the stairs, which led off to the right. He rubbed his hand across the stubble on his chin and looked at the framed certificate awarded to Juan Calbo for his work over the year at school in grade 4. People with kids didn't know how lucky they were: they left behind them something of themselves when they died. Juana-Marie had been able to leave nothing but memories and a few fading photographs.

Catalina came down the stairs and Alvarez's admiration was immediate and respectful. Dressed very neatly, her jet-black hair drawn tightly back into a bun, she moved with natural grace. He introduced himself, quickly put her at her ease, and began to question her.

'How did the señora get on with the señor?' she said, as she sat down on a rush-seated chair and motioned him to sit on a second one. 'But very well. What else would you expect?'

'I'm not in a position to expect anything, Señora, which is why I'm asking. There were no rows between them?'

'Rows? But the señora was very fond of him.'

'And he of her?'

'Undoubtedly.'

'And you didn't notice any change in his attitude towards her during the last week?'

'The last week?' She thought back. 'During the last week before she died, I didn't see them.'

'Neither of them?'

'They were out on picnics. The car was gone, the key of the house was behind the outside door, and I knew what to do. On the Friday, my money was in an envelope stuck to the window of the kitchen, as it always was when the señora was out for the day.'

'Then when exactly did you actually last see them?'

'I suppose it was the middle of the previous week. With the kind of weather we've been having, wouldn't you have been out on picnics?'

'Of course,' he answered. How the rich lived, he thought resentfully. But he had to acknowledge that as Tatham had driven round the countryside he must have studied the fields, assessed the state of the crops, sympathized with those who needed capital to break out of a primitive form of agriculture or horticulture, hated those who were responsible for the creeping housing developments, and he could no longer feel truly resentful.

She looked straight at him. 'Why are you asking these questions?'

'We have to ask many questions after such an accident,' he answered brusquely. 'Has anything at all unusual recently taken place in the house? Has anything altered?'

He noticed her expression of uncertainty. 'Señora, please tell me what has been unusual.' He allowed a slight note of command to slip into his voice.

She fidgeted with her hands, running thumb and forefinger of one hand up and down the middle finger of the other. 'But it's all so stupid ...'

'I still wish to hear.'

'The señora wore old dresses and sometimes looked like — like a gypsy — but that was her business, you understands But she was very fussy about her pyjamas and changed them twice a week, every week. She left me to make her bed, so I know. But just recently, she has worn the same pyjamas for days and days.'

It seemed a matter of no importance, since it could have no bearing on whether or not she'd been murdered. But to give her confidence, he praised Catalina. 'You are very observant, Señora, and are helping a great deal. Now, has there been anything else?'

'Only the deep-freeze, which I've this moment recalled.'

'Tell me about that.'

'It was locked for several days, which it's never been before.'

He looked at her, without realizing it, in a speculative manner.

'No,' she said sharply, 'I do not steal food from it. In the whole of my life I have never stolen a peseta's worth of anything. But I was curious to see what the señora ate and what it cost her and I used often to look inside.'

'I never thought otherwise,' he lied.

She relaxed, accepting his denial as genuine. 'When it was once more unlocked, all the food had changed.'

'Perhaps they had a big party?' he suggested in an offhand manner.

'The señora did not give parties. But if she had have done, she'd have asked me to help. And what kind of a party would use fish, meat, vegetables, fruit, cream, and ice-cream, all at the same time? There was another thing. When the new food was put in, there was quite a lot of squid. The señora did not like squid.'

'But perhaps the señor did?'

'He said not, when I asked him how he liked our food.'

He had, he thought, learned something about their eating habits, but nothing towards proving Tatham had murdered his great-aunt.

Catalina smoothed down her dress with her long, shapely lingers whose skin had not been roughened by all the housework she did. 'The señora was a strange woman, but she was very kind and she loved our country.' She shook her head slowly. 'She was much nicer than other people I work for and who dress smartly and it was very sad it was her who fell.'

'Very sad,' he agreed. 'Tell me something. Wasn't it a bit odd, going out in the evening at that time to look for a plant instead of waiting for the next day?'

'Odd for her? Never. When she heard about a plant she hadn't seen, she was like a man with a sweetheart in the next village — time meant nothing. I remember ...'

He listened and was convinced that there was nothing basically illogical in Elvina Woods's actions just prior to her death.

Alvarez was becoming hungry, so he went into the small bar near the travel agents in Puerto Llueso and ordered a brandy. The barman asked for twenty pesetas. Alvarez identified himself and then said that a brandy in Llueso cost him five pesetas and he wasn't paying tourist prices for anyone. The barman shrugged his shoulders and told Alvarez to have it on the house.

Alvarez finished his drink and then went into the tourist agency. The man and the woman who worked in it were preparing to close for lunch, but they resignedly settled down to answering his questions.

'Do you know Señor Tatham?' he asked them both. 'He is an Englishman who may have come in here to buy an air ticket for his aunt, Señora Woods? It would have been a ticket to England.'

The woman moved her handbag to one side, opened a drawer, and brought out a form which was half filled in. She ran a pencil down the entries until she found the one she sought. 'Yes,' she said, without looking up, 'he came here and bought a ticket to London.'

'How much was it?'

'Eight thousand three hundred pesetas.'

'Can you remember how he paid? By cheque or by cash?'

'With cash.'

The man spoke nervously. 'The money's all right, isn't it? It's not counterfeit?'

'No. There are no problems like that.'

'That's a mercy.'

'D'you mind if I use a phone?' Alvarez said. He leaned over and picked up the receiver that was in front of the woman. When he'd briefly looked through the handbag in the Fiat 128, he'd noticed that the cheque-book inside was for the Caja de Ahorros y Monte de Piedad de las Baleares, Puerto Llueso branch. He asked the operator to give him the bank and as he waited he wondered whether the automatic exchange would ever open. The call was put through and he asked the man he spoke to to make certain there was someone in the bank in five minutes' time. The man said the bank didn't close until two.

He drove from the travel agent along the front, past a swarm of noisy French tourists who had just disembarked from a bus, turned left, and parked in the square.

The bank manager, a smiling man in his middle forties, came forward and he recognized Alvarez. They shook hands across the counter and exchanged brief courtesies, then Alvarez said: 'I'd like some information on Señora Elvina Woods's account.'

'The lady who so unfortunately died? Is there some sort of trouble?'

'Possibly, possibly not,' said Alvarez vaguely. 'The first question is, did, she withdraw more than eight thousand pesetas last Friday?'

'I'll check the two accounts — she has an ordinary one and still a sum of money in a convertible one.' The manager chuckled. 'Head Office keep telling me to try to get her to liquidate the convertible one and I reply each time that she is not a woman to be persuaded. Wasn't, I should say.' He went over to a filing cabinet and slid out a drawer, rifled through the filing cards and extracted two 'Last Friday …? The twenty-fifth …? No, there were no withdrawals on either account.'

'When was her last one?'

The manager checked the first card. 'Back on the fourteenth.'

'That's quite a time before she died.'

'Eleven days.'

'Is that odd?'

The manager fingered his chin. 'She never drew regularly on the same day each week. But she usually drew more often than this.'

'What was her last withdrawal for?'

He consulted the card again. 'Five thousand. That was what she usually withdrew.'

'What did her weekly withdrawal work out at?'

'In cash? There was a cheque once a month for rent, though it was pretty small.'

'Yes, in cash.'

The manager picked up a pencil and worked out some figures. 'About three thousand nine hundred.'

Alvarez thought about that figure. 'D'you know her nephew? Senor Tatham?'

'She introduced him when he first came to the island and said we must give him a good rate of exchange. I told her, for travellers' cheques, there is only the one rate, but I don't think she believed me.' The manager smiled. 'A very definite woman.'

'Did he cash any travellers' cheques on Friday, the twenty-fifth?'

The manager left the counter and spoke to the two other men who worked in the bank. The younger of the two crossed to another filing cabinet and checked through a bundle of forms. After half a minute, he pulled one free. 'He cashed cheques for a hundred pounds on the Friday.'

Alvarez made a note of the amount. 'Thanks for all your help.'

'It's nothing,' replied the manager.

Alvarez left the corner building and returned to his car, but did not immediately start the engine. He'd been given no absolute proof that Tatham had bought that ticket with his own money, but all the available evidence said that he had. Why, unless the señora was not alive to pay for it herself?

*

Tatham walked up the road to Ca'n Xema as the sun dipped below the mountain behind the Creyola/Llueso road.

Judy was in, on her own, and she made no secret of the fact that she was delighted to see him. 'I've been listening to Tchaikovsky's Fifth and getting more and more depressed, so you've got to cheer me up.'

'Why depressed by music like that?'

'Because it heightens whatever mood I'm in when I start to listen and I was thoroughly depressed to start with. I should have tried Wagner. He annoys me so much with his old superman mythology that I forget myself.'

'So what depressed you in the first case?'

She hesitated, but her need to talk was too great. 'I'm scared of something that's happening.'

'Here, in this house? It is something that Lawrence is doing?'

She nodded.

He spoke quietly. 'Is it financial? Elvina used to say that he was the kind of man who'd always sail a little too close to the wind, so that one day he'd get capsized.'

'It's kind of financial. And I'm terribly fond of him and can't bear to think of him getting into real trouble.' She nibbled her lower lip.

'Do you have any idea exactly what's up?'

'Not really. Only that he's been short of money for some time and recently the government's been pressing him for taxes he owes so things really are getting tight. He was terribly worried — until he interested a German, Naupert, in buying this house.'

'What's wrong with that?'

'He's persuaded Naupert to agree to pay five million more than the place is worth, yet the German is a very hard-headed businessman.'

'The hardest head can sometimes do something stupid when he steps outside his own line of business. This Naupert could have liked the house so much he just never bothered to find out what its market value is.'

'That isn't possible — he even had two German surveyors flown over from Essen to check the place. He'll have consulted the market and know to the last peseta what this place is worth. He's willing to pay five million more because …' She stopped.

'Because?' he prompted.

'Because of the Renoir in the sitting-room,' she said in a rush. 'That painting suddenly appeared and it was obviously because Naupert was coming to the house — he's a well-known art connoisseur and collector.'

'But it can't be genuine. If so, it would be worth much more than Lawrence is asking for the whole place.'

'I know it can't be genuine. But I think Naupert's being led to believe it is. I think Larry is ...' Again she stopped.

Was Ingham so hard pressed for money he was trying to sell a faked Renoir? But that failed to make sense, thought Tatham. If no more than five million was indirectly being asked for the painting, it couldn't be being offered as genuine. But suppose it was the other way round? Sold as an acknowledged fake to a buyer who believed it genuine? The oldest gambit in the confidence trickster's book: apparently giving the victim the chance to make a lot of money by appealing to the sense of larceny that was said to lie in every man's soul. He explained this to Judy.

Without speaking, she led the way out of the music-room into the sitting-room and stood in front of the Renoir. It was an attractive painting, he thought, vaguely familiar, though he was far too ignorant of art to be able to name it.

'Suppose he is playing it like that?' said Judy in a low voice. 'Is he doing anything legally wrong?'

'Under Spanish law? I haven't the slightest idea what the answer really is, but I'd guess that if Lawrence called it a fake from the beginning and no one could prove that he's overpricing the house because he expects the German to be misled into believing the painting is genuine, then no. After all, when you sell any house you always start by asking more than it's worth.'

'You really think that?'

'Yes.'

'Thank God,' she murmured, as if his opinion were good law. 'I don't know why I didn't think of Larry's doing it that way round: just got panicky, I suppose. It's so like him. Making money as he makes a fool out of an expert. No wonder he's been so cheerful!' She turned and her voice sharpened. 'John, you won't breathe a word about this to anyone, will you?'

'What d'you take me for?' he protested.

'Sorry, but gossiping is the busiest occupation after boozing out here ... And talking about drink, will you have one?'

'Of course. That was my sole reason for coming along.'

She smiled for the first time. 'Then I'll pour out two very large drinks, turn on Brahms loud and clear, and in next to no time I'll be feeling relaxed, comfortable, and human.'

'Were you aware that cows give more milk to Brahms than to pop?'

'You know something? Until right now, that's one of the facts of life I've been able to live without.'

CHAPTER XIX

THE CORPORAL was in the captain's office — the captain rarely arrived before eleven in the morning — sorting through the papers on the desk when through the open doorway he saw Alvarez go by. 'Hey! Enrique, Where the hell have you been?'

Alvarez returned to lean against the jamb. His shirt had a stain down it where he had spilled some soup the previous evening: his trousers were virtually without creases: he'd shaved badly and there was a noticeable triangle of stubble on the right-hand side of his chin.

'I'll swear,' said the corporal, 'you look like you died during the night.'

'I did. So now I'm going to go and lie down.'

'Like hell you are. You are going to be one very busy man. There's been someone on the telephone, demanding to speak to you at once, pronto, appassionato.'

'Did you tell him I was out in the field, working myself to a crop of ulcers?'

'I said you were probably in bed, snoring, too pissed to do anything else.'

'Great. Remind me to do you a favour some day.' Alvarez took a pack of cigarettes from his pocket and lit one. Three guards walked past and one loudly demanded to know why the previous day's rubbish hadn't been removed.

'Don't you want to know who's called?' asked the corporal.

'No.'

'You're the laziest, sleepiest bastard I've ever met.'

'Then you don't know my brother. He hasn't crawled out of bed in the past five years.'

The corporal straightened up and moved away from the desk. 'The bloke who wants you is a regular hidalgo, all orders and do-as-I-tell-you-chum-or-else. A professor of anatomy, he calls himself. God help those who get anatomized by him.'

'Quite,' said Alvarez drily. 'Since they're dead, they won't get help from anyone else.' He jerked himself upright and left, climbed the stairs past the peeling plaster, and reached his room. He sat down and yawned. Too much work. All his own bloody stupid fault. He lit a cigarette, decided he was feeling even lousier than before, opened the bottom drawer of the desk and poured himself out a brandy. On his desk were two letters which had arrived that morning. Forms on which certain statistics were to be entered. He threw them into the waste-paper basket. The telephone rang. A woman with a twittering voice said he'd turned up at last, had he?, and Professor Goñi had been waiting for hours to speak to him. He hooked the receiver up on his shoulder, leaned back in the chair, and rested his feet on the desk as he waited for the great professor to come on the line. Through the window, he saw a young woman walking along the narrow pavement and the way she swung her hips made him feel randy for the first time in days.

'This is Professor Goñi,' said a voice with a Madrid lisp.

Alvarez identified himself. He apologized for not having been at the station before, but said he'd been working since daybreak.

'It has caused me considerable inconvenience to have repeatedly to try to contact you,' said the professor.

He apologized again.

'I wish you to know that I have completed my initial post-mortem on the deceased, Señora Woods. There are several points of interest to observe, though you will please treat as provisional only any information I give you now. Is that clear?'

Alvarez said it was quite clear. He pictured the professor in a knife-edged suit, newly laundered white shirt, tightly knotted tie, shining leather shoes. He removed his feet from the desk, let the chair fall down to a normal upright position, reached down, and refilled his glass.

'The deceased was a woman whose general physical condition as far as this could be determined was consistent with her age. Her injuries were very extensive, with many fractured bones and ruptured internal organs. The nature of some of these injuries is at the moment a little … mystifying.' He spoke the word with distaste.

Alvarez put the glass down on the desk. 'How so, Professor?'

There was a long technical explanation. He understood few of the individual words, but gained the general meaning: the injuries were in part less extreme, in part more extreme, than might have been expected, and they were in nature unusual.

'It was a very considerable drop,' he said.

'Having read the report, I am well aware of that fact.'

Alvarez shrugged his shoulders. He lit a cigarette.

Further points. The deceased had lost an ear, ripped off without the kind of tearing to be expected: the injury bore signs of having occurred after death, but due to the general state of the head and the immersion for several days in sea-water, this could not be stated with absolute certainty: there were very extensive injuries to the top of her skull, but one segment of bone had survived relatively intact and this bore the marks of a blow from a blunt object about two centimetres in width.

'Not from a piece of rock?' queried Alvarez.

It couldn't be stated that explicitly. Rock of a certain shape, for instance, with a crest to it, could just conceivably have caused this particular injury.

'But also so could a stick of some sort?'

Quite so. But no certainty. Further points. Putrefaction had set in, with characteristic discoloration at root of the neck and on the face and the face was swollen — decomposition appeared to have taken place very rapidly in the five days between death and the post-mortem, but the temperature of the sea had been on the high side, at nearly seventeen degrees centigrade, and this probably explained the fact and in any case the degree of advance of decomposition was notoriously open to wide variations. The deceased had died some two hours after a light meal, mainly of bread, and there was no discernible alcohol in her blood which meant that if she'd experienced the normal rate of absorption — and there was no reason to suppose she hadn't — she had not taken alcohol for at least nine hours. A chip of concrete, no bigger than half a centimetre by a quarter, had been embedded in her skull.

'Concrete?'

Had his words not been explicitly clear? The professor would ring again should there be any more definite information to give and would the detective this time please be handy to take the call. The line went dead.

Alvarez flicked ash on to the floor. That report almost certainly confirmed murder. He sighed. Now, there was no avoiding fate. People would be down from Palma, poking their noses into everything, looking everywhere, questioning everyone, and his previous privacy would be shattered once and for all. The English, he thought miserably, would destroy Heaven if, by some grave oversight, any of them were ever allowed to enter.

*

Alvarez loathed heights with all the bowel-gripping terror of someone who had suffered from a fear of them since childhood. But he also had the kind of stubborn character which refused in the final event to give in to such fear because that would have been acknowledging a weakness he was not prepared to acknowledge.

He stood by the side of the Land-Rover parked near to the edge of the cliff at the point where Señora Woods had gone over, stared at the onlookers who were being kept back by two guards, and knew he'd have given his all to change places with any of them, even the English queer at the right.

'Here's your harness,' said someone.

He fitted it over his shoulders and clipped it tight. Sweet Mary, he prayed, don't let the webbing be rotted so that it parts. One of the three municipal policemen who'd arrived in the Land-Rover connected the wire from the front-mounted winch to his harness with a shackle. Sweet Jesus, he prayed, don't let the shackle pin work loose or the wire fray and part.

'You look like you were dressing up for your own funeral,' said the policeman and laughed.

Lord, prayed Alvarez, if I do crash to my hideous death, send down a bolt of lightning to bum up this fool.

As he went over the edge, fear blanketed his mind and loosened his bladder so that he urinated very briefly. The cliff face was at first sheer, then it bulged out into a small shelf after which it became sheer once more. His feet landed on the bulge and he made the awful mistake of looking down. The world swayed and there was a roaring in his ears; he heard the harness begin to tear, the shackle pin to unwind, the steel wire to fray. Sweat rolled down his face and body. Death could be nothing but a thrice-welcome relief.

The point at which Señora Woods had struck the bulge was macabrely marked by her ear which was now shrivelled and beginning to decompose badly. With trembling hands, he collected it up into a plastic bag. He put the bag in his pocket and examined the bulge, trying as he did so not to look down again into the space beneath. Nowhere was there a clearly defined ridge about two centimetres in width, nor was there a single chip of concrete.

'Haul me up,' he shouted.

They hauled him up and as he scrambled over the rim and his feet touched solid ground, he could have wept with relief.

*

Back in his room in the station and two brandies later. Alvarez read the note on his desk. Señora Pino at the forensic laboratory in Palma would like him to ring her. He did so.

'Do you know anything about inks?' she asked him.

'No, señora, nothing at all.' She sounded warm and nice and cuddly: someone to curl up with after the most horrifying experience of one's life.

'They're quite interesting in some respects and very infuriating in others.' She launched enthusiastically into a learned dissertation on inks. The age of ink could seldom be determined with any degree of success, except when of the gallotannic type and even then no degree of accuracy could really be guaranteed. There were three main types of inks: gallotannic, chromic, and aniline. Each type was capable of innumerable compositions which could not probably be differentiated. All the marks in the book of plants with one exception had been made in a chromic ink. The exception, marks concerning *Scutellaria balearica*, had been made in a gallotannic ink only a very few days prior to examination. Despite many tests of various natures, no further information of any value had come to light.

He thanked her.

'Just one final thing, señor. I was interested enough to have a word with a friend of mine who's quite a good botanist. He says that no one with the slightest knowledge and experience of plants on this island would look for *Scutellaria balearica* up on the mountains between Llueso and Parelona. The local climate's all wrong and the height is wrong.'

He thanked her again and rang off. Nothing definite ... yet strong confirmation of a kind.

*

As Alvarez drew up alongside the garage at Ca'n Manin, Tatham came round from the front door of the house. Alvarez looked down at the small, battered plastic container on the front passenger seat, hesitated, then left it there. He climbed out. 'I apologize for troubling you yet again, señor, but there are still one or two questions to ask you.'

Tatham could not hide his immediate sense of unease, even fear. 'More questions still? I thought you'd come to tell me that I'd at last got permission to arrange the funeral?'

'I'm afraid that on this island everything moves slowly.'

'Except burials,' he replied. 'Aren't they usually within twenty-four hours of death?'

'Everything will surely be in order soon. May we sit down for a while? Out here, in the sun? I spend so much time in an office that it is nice to be out in the open.'

They sat at the garden table and the wind-rustled vine leaves sent dancing shadows over them.

Alvarez spoke quietly. 'You and your aunt had a picnic on Friday, I believe?'

'Yes.'

'What did you eat?'

'How on earth can that matter?'

'Señor, if you knew the absurd details I have to file if a person so much as loses a camera ...' Alvarez shrugged his shoulders in a gesture of resigned hopelessness.

Tatham accepted the explanation he'd been given. 'Chicken, ham, bread, cheese, tomatoes, a couple of yoghurts ... The usual sort of food.'

'But nothing to drink?'

'You didn't know my aunt!' He spoke easily, his previous fears suppressed because this was a story rehearsed so many times. 'She reckoned a meal without wine wasn't a proper meal.'

'So what did she have?'

'I don't remember exactly, but it must have been a couple of vermouths and at least a couple of glasses of wine.'

'And when you returned here from the picnic, she left immediately to search for that plant with a long Latin name?'

'That's right.'

'She had no tea?'

Obviously some special significance held to the food and drink she'd consumed, but it was impossible to guess what. Therefore, he had to stick exactly with the story he'd previously given. 'She wouldn't even wait for a cup of coffee. When she was on the track of a new plant, she waited for nothing.' He surreptitiously stared at the detective, but could make out nothing from the other's somewhat gloomy expression.

Alvarez lit a cigarette. The dead woman had, according to the P.M., eaten a light meal without alcohol two hours before her death and had consumed no alcohol within nine hours of death. Tatham was lying about the picnic. 'Señor,' he said pleasantly, 'are you quite certain you have told me exactly how everything happened on that Friday?'

The shock of knowing his story was obviously disbelieved scrambled Tatham's mind so that for a time he could not even try to answer.

Alvarez stood up, pushing back the garden chair so that it scraped across the rough concrete with an irritating noise. 'Would you object if I ask to examine the back of the Fiat in the garage?'

'Do ... do what?' asked Tatham stupidly.

Alvarez repeated the question.

'Why d'you want to do that?'

Alvarez's tone of voice didn't change. 'To try to determine whether you have at any time carried the body of the señora in it.'

They stared at each other and Tatham belatedly realized that he was suspected of killing Elvina. 'You don't really think ... But you can't think I'd kill her.'

'Señor, I know for certain nothing, but I have many things I must investigate. That is why I ask for your permission to examine your car.' He was now taking great care to be courteous, a rare event and, had Tatham realized it, a very ominous one.

'You'll be wasting your time,' said Tatham hoarsely.

'Time is plentiful,' replied Alvarez. He stood up, waited to see if Tatham was going to say anything more, then went over to his car and picked up from the front seat the battered suitcase which contained certain equipment which included that necessary for determining traces of blood.

He put the suitcase down behind the Fiat, lifted the tailgate. The dead woman had been small, but even so the back seat would have had to be folded flat in order to cany her. He went round and opened the passenger door, released the catch of the front seat and tilted it up, climbed into the back and lowered the back of the back seat. Tatham came and stood by the car, obviously nervous, obviously worried.

Before leaving the station, Alvarez had read through a text-book in his office and this had reminded him of facts, forgotten until now, once learned at the police college. Dried bloodstains were very frequently difficult to detect, especially since they often did not look like bloodstains on certain backgrounds. But, even in daytime, their discovery was made easier by the use of artificial light when they might appear as patches of glossy varnish.

He switched on a powerful torch and shone it across the loading platform, slowly moving it in an arc. For a long time he saw nothing, then there was a hint of something up by the right-hand wheel arch. He raised the torch and brought it nearer and now he could make out an irregular, glossy stain about two centimetres long.

He took from the suitcase a glass rod, two plastic tubes filled with liquid, and a filter paper. Tatham, he noticed, was now very disturbed. He soaked the filter paper with the reagent from the second bottle, took the glass rod and dipped it in the first bottle which contained distilled water, then pressed the rod against the near end of the stain for several seconds. He lifted the rod off and placed it on the filter paper. Almost immediately, a green stain appeared. He began to return the equipment to the suitcase. After a short while, he said: 'Señor, there are traces of blood in the rear of this car. Can you explain them?'

Tatham vividly recalled how he'd wrapped the body in the bedcover and put it in the car. Obviously, a small piece of frozen blood had broken off and then melted through to the vinyl-type covering. Yet traces of blood on their own could prove nothing …

'I regret that this car must be taken to Palma to be examined by experts, who will determine whether the blood is human in origin.' Alvarez lowered the tailgate.

'What are you really saying?' demanded Tatham, although nothing could be more obvious.

'I am not satisfied that Señora Woods died in a fall at the point in the mountains where this car was found.'

'But where else could she have …?'

'Señor.' Alvarez lit a cigarette. 'It is no good arguing with me. Now, everything is handed over to Palma, where there are very much keener brains than mine.' He drew on the cigarette, then said angrily: 'And Palma will undoubtedly send out a team of experts who will come here and solve the many problems which I find unsolvable.'

'What problems? What's unsolvable?'

Alvarez sighed. Why must the Englishman go on and on when it must be obvious to him that it was all over? 'Your aunt was small for an Englishwoman, was she not?'

'I suppose she was, yes.'

'You have told me that when you returned from the picnic she drove from here to look for a flower?'

'Yes, that's what happened.'

'When I sat in the Fiat, up in the mountains, the driving seat was set so far back that I could not properly work the controls with my feet and I could not see clearly in the mirror, yet the señora was the same size as me. The last person to drive the Fiat was not the señora.'

That he could have been so incredibly stupid! thought Tatham, with sick despair.

'You told me you had a picnic together, with chicken and ham and cheese, and so on, and plenty to drink. Yet the señora died two hours after a light meal, mainly of bread, and she had not drunk alcohol for many hours.'

'I ... She had a very quick tea ...' began Tatham desperately.

Alvarez shook his head. 'You told me exactly. She would not stop long enough even to have some coffee. She had to find the flower.'

Tatham remembered how he'd stressed her desire to be off.

'The señora, in addition to her other injuries, received a blow from something round and strong, about two centimetres in diameter. I examined the cliff face where she fell and there was no formation of rock which could have caused such an injury. Also, there was a small piece of cement wedged in her skull: nowhere on the cliff face could she have picked up that piece of cement. Her ear was torn off on a small bulge of rock. Expert evidence says the ear was removed after death, yet had she fallen alive over that cliff, she could not have been dead when she hit the bulge.'

And he'd been so confident there were no traces of what had really happened.

'You told me the señora was looking for a particular plant. Yet an expert says that no one with any knowledge of the plants of this island would look for that in the mountains between Puerto Llueso and Parelona.'

What other incredibly stupid mistakes had he made?

'It was you who bought the ticket for the flight to London, not the señora.'

He tried to fight on. 'She asked me to get it.'

'And did she give you the money to pay for it?'

'She gave me the cash.'

'Yet the señora had drawn no cash from her bank for many days, so many days that it is inconceivable she should have had eight thousand three hundred pesetas left. But you cashed travellers' cheques for one hundred pounds before going to the travel agency.'

'She ... she said that she'd give me a cheque when I got back.'

'What stopped her, for she gave you no such cheque? You returned and handed her the ticket, didn't you? It was in her handbag.'

'It somehow got forgotten.'

'The señora was a rich woman, was she not?'

'No. She had only a life interest in her money.'

'But on the Friday morning a cable arrived to tell her her godfather had died and he was exceedingly wealthy and he left her his money.'

'I ... I believe so. I mean, yes, the cable came.'

'And you were made heir to the señora's estate by a new will?'

'I don't know. She didn't discuss that with me. What is it? D'you think I killed her for her money? After she'd been so kind to me out here? Even though I liked her so much?'

'Someone killed, or seriously injured, her by hitting her over the head with a blunt weapon. She was then carried in the Fiat up into the mountains and dropped over the edge to make her death seem accidental.'

'You've got it hopelessly wrong.'

'How else did the blood get into the back of the Fiat? How else did a small piece of yellow thread also get into the back, a thread which came off one of the bedcovers — all of which I shall take away — unless that was what she was wrapped up in?'

Tatham slumped down in a garden chair. He stared out at the orange trees bathed in the hot sunshine, and at the monastery perched on top of its conical hill. He'd left a trail a mile long. They'd plot it out exactly, but with one vital mistake: they'd nail him for the murder. A vast estate to provide motive, a fall over the cliff that could be proved to have been faked, a car in which there was the blood of the dead woman ...

Alvarez sat down opposite him. When he spoke, his voice was soft and persuasive. 'Señor, why not tell the truth and so ease your conscience? A man can't escape his conscience, ever. Believe me, it will be so much easier for you.'

He could exonerate himself from everything but the offence of concealing Elvina's death by confessing, yet to confess was to lose that farm ... He had no choice. 'Several months ago,' he began slowly, 'my fiancée was murdered because the law couldn't protect her although it had promised to do so ...'

CHAPTER XX

ALVAREZ DRANK some of the brandy recently poured out for him. He looked across the table and saw an expression of bleak, bitter resignation on Tatham's face and that, as much as anything, convinced him he'd heard the truth.

He finished the brandy and poured himself out a refill. He lit one cigarette from the stub of the first. He too stared out across the land. He saw the small garden, the orange grove, the land which should have been under cultivation but wasn't. And he knew the primitive desire, that came from his parents and their parents, to own land, to let it trickle through his fingers, to work it and make it yield crops. Had he been this Englishman, faced with similar circumstances, he would have done the same thing, if more expertly. What man of the soil would have hesitated? To conceal a death for a few days was nothing, to own land everything.

He remembered many facts, some of which he had not concerned himself with because they'd seemed unimportant, but which now slotted into place. The dead woman had been dressed in clothes for cold weather, not hot: it had been cold in the middle of the month. The gap between the death of the godfather and the apparent death of the señora had been so narrow because it had to be: had she been alive she would have flown to England for the funeral. Catalina had not seen the señora for days, but had accepted she was just on a picnic: yet the señora's pyjamas had not been changed twice a week as they had always been previously. The deep-freeze had been locked for several days which normally never happened and the food had all been changed: some of the frozen food was of a kind neither the señora nor the Englishman liked. The señora had drawn no money after the fourteenth, although normally she must have done. The blow to the head had been caused by the bamboo on to which she had fallen head first. The chip of concrete had come from the patio …

He drained his glass and stood up. 'Show me where you found her,' he ordered.

Tatham showed him where the body of Elvina had lain. Alvarez squatted on his heels and examined the base of the concrete pillar, which was stepped in three folds: on the middle step, the concrete had weathered badly and had broken up into innumerable pieces, both small and large.

Tatham had said he'd washed everything down very thoroughly, but a test would probably disclose the presence of blood. Alvarez moved his head, preparatory to rising to his feet, and he caught a minute flick of light: a detailed examination disclosed a single brown-grey hair which had become wedged under an edge of concrete. He very carefully withdrew it and placed it on his handkerchief. It was about the same shade as the dead woman's hair had been and certainly was not the colour of Tatham's hair.

They went into the house and upstairs to the balcony where the repairs to the wooden rails were obvious when specifically looked for. It had been raining on the night she'd died. The balcony had an uneven surface and this would have allowed puddles to collect over pockets of dust and dirt. She had come out during a break in the rain to get a breath of fresh air, to look out at the bay, to enjoy the mountains when wet as their character changed so much, and she'd moved forward, her foot had slipped in one of the puddles, she'd grabbed the rails to catch herself as they, rotten, had given way. She'd fallen head first on to the bamboo and the concrete.

'I want to see the deep-freeze,' he said.

Tatham silently led the way downstairs, through the sitting-room and kitchen, out to the wash-room.

The deep-freeze was only a quarter full. Alvarez asked Tatham to empty it whilst he collected his suitcase of equipment from his car. On his return, he switched on the torch, leaned over, and shone it round the inside. The sides were quite heavily frosted, but the bottom was free and in one corner the beam of the torch picked out a small patch of 'varnish'. He tested this with glass rod, filter paper, and reagent, and the filter paper turned green where the rod had touched it.

'OK,' said Alvarez, 'let's get the food back in.' He repacked the suitcase before helping to replace the food.

When everything was back in the cabinet, he said: 'Will you take me out to where you threw the food?'

Tatham led the way into the shed next door, which had once housed pigs, and through that into the scrubland beyond: land far too rocky to have been farmable even in the days when labour had been so cheap. Ironically, now the land was valuable for building purposes.

They pushed past low, thorny shrubs, evergreen oaks, and the occasional pine tree, and came to an area where the largest boulders were over two metres high. 'It was somewhere here,' said Tatham, 'but I was in such a hell of a state that I can't remember exactly where.'

Two green dragonflies swept past, wings and bodies sparkling in the sun; a small flock of non-feral pigeons wheeled overhead. From the urbanization on the mountain to the north-east came the echoing blast of two explosions as more foundation trenches were blasted out of the rock.

'Can you smell something?' said Alvarez, as he sniffed.

'Only the wild herbs.'

'I am smelling something very unlike herbs.' Alvarez turned to his left and scaled a large boulder, sniffed again, checked the direction of the breeze and walked forward. 'Here we are,' he shouted.

Tatham crossed a patch of open land, bent to get under the lowest branches of an oak, and picked up the smell of rotting as he stepped clear. He pushed past a stunted algar-roba tree to stand next to Alvarez. Heaped around several bushes were the remains of the food he had thrown out from the deep-freeze: much of it was maggotty, all of it was stinking.

They returned to the old pig barn, went through and into the house, from there back out to the patio. Alvarez sat down and poured himself out a brandy. He stared out at the land.

What now? wondered Tatham dully. A full statement, more questioning by other detectives, a further autopsy to test his latest story, a charge of obstructing justice? A letter to the British authorities to say an attempt had been made to falsify the date of Señora Woods's death and that this had actually occurred on the sixteenth of April? Eight days before Maitland died.

'Señor,' said Alvarez slowly and carefully, 'I believe you when you tell me what really happened. Because I feel you do not lie now. And because there was that hair on the pillar, the broken wooden rails above, the blood in the deepfreeze. But above all because why would you kill the señora before Señor Maitland died, knowing you would have to keep her death a secret? If you were going to kill her, it must surely have been some little time afterwards when her death would not be directly connected with Señor Maitland's death and when an "accident" could be arranged and the body found without the dangerous need to store it in the deep-freeze. And if you are speaking all of the truth and she had told you she was going to leave you some or all of the money she inherited, why run the risk of killing her at all? No, señor, you did not murder her.'

'I hope to God your seniors agree.'

'My seniors.' Alvarez ran the nail of his thumb across the stubble of his chin with a rasping sound. The sun slipped below the level of the vine to dazzle his eyes and he moved the chair to escape the direct rays. The Englishman had complained that justice had betrayed him and killed his fiancée. Justice so often did betray people. If there were real justice in the world, good people would not suffer. Yet Juana-Marie, who was only good, had been made to suffer.

No, there was no real justice in the world.

His superior chief in Palma would never understand about earth: that it could give a man a sensual thrill as it trickled through his fingers. His superior chief would order a full investigation and then send the finalized details to England so that 'justice' should be done. Justice here would mean the Englishman would be deprived of his farm and the money would go to people who were already rich enough and would spend this extra on such things as holiday villas which destroyed all beauty and dispossessed farmers.

The sun dipped behind the mountain and the shadows raced across the land, covering fruit trees, crops, workers in the fields with bent backs, mules endlessly tilling the soil. 'You have a telephone, señor?'

'Yes. In the sitting-room.'

'Wait here, please.' Alvarez went through to the sitting-room. He lifted the receiver, asked the operator for Palma, and was put through inside five minutes. He spoke to Professor Goñi.

The professor had conducted a further post-mortem examination, but had nothing more to report. The injuries were unusual, but since few people fell into water from such heights and were washed around for days it was not easy to judge the significance of the injuries by meaningful comparisons. The question of some of the injuries having occurred after death must be borne in mind, especially remembering the ear, but a body floating in the sea near to shore, especially when submerged before the gases took it to the surface, must frequently be pounded against rocks and it was very difficult indeed to judge the effect of this as opposed to injuries inflicted after death but before immersion.

'The body showed no signs of having been subjected to some unusual process?'

What was that supposed to mean? The body had been subjected to a very long — and skilful — examination and a full report had been given.

Alvarez thanked the professor, who seemed to suspect his professional competency had been put in doubt, rang off, and returned outside to the patio.

Tatham looked up. He spoke in a hopeless voice. 'Do you want me to come into Llueso now? May I get in touch with the British consul first and explain what's happened?'

'I think,' said Alvarez quietly, as he sat down, 'the best thing you can do is not to say anything to anybody. Do you mind if I have another small brandy?' He poured himself out a very large one.

Tatham stared at him and wondered whether he understood what had really been said?

CHAPTER XXI

ALVAREZ SAT in his office, elbows resting on the cluttered desk, and read with interest the relevant passage in G. P. Ross's book, *Forensic Medicine for the Layman*, translated from the original English nine years before. 'Some loss of detail of body cells' structure should be apparent on microscopic examination after a body has been completely frozen and has then been thawed out (it must be remembered, as was stated in chapter seven, that a temperature well below — 18° C, or 0° F, is needed if a body is to be preserved for any length of time). But this loss of detail is easily missed, especially if there be any accompanying gross physical damage, unless the investigator has been informed that freezing, or its possibility, took place. The only other indication is the too rapid decomposition which is sometimes occasioned. If the time between death and the finding of the body is known exactly and the state of decomposition is advanced well beyond that normally to be expected, a previous state of freezing may be suspected. But it must again be emphasized that the degree of decomposition is at all times so variable that this on its own must not be taken as a reliable guide.'

He closed the text-book with a snap. Soon, he would telephone the superior chief's office and report that his investigations now confirmed the accident had taken place as originally reported so that permission for the funeral could be given. There would be a few sharp words over the waste of funds occasioned by the unnecessary post-mortem, but it would eventually blow over. And surely anyone so incompetent as to make a mystery of a perfectly ordinary accident was fit only for leaving in a backwater where nothing of real importance ever happened and his incompetence could do no harm?

He let the chair fall back until it rested against the wall and put his feet up on the desk. He undid the top two buttons of his shirt and scratched his hairy chest where it tickled. He closed his eyes. He'd never seen a large dairy farm in England, or anywhere else for that matter, but he thought he could visualize it with reasonable accuracy … Except for the grass which reputedly grew as high as a house because it rained almost every day of the year …

When Tatham arrived at Ca'n Xema, Judy opened the front door. 'Hallo, John. Come on in. Larry's on the phone, but he'll be with us soon.' She studied him. 'You look like … almost as if you'd just seen a ghost.'

'Maybe I did.' His voice was gay: he was feeling lightheaded from relief. 'But if I did, it turned out to be a friendly ghost.'

'Whatever that might really mean, I prescribe a further dose of spirits. Come on into the sitting-room.'

As they entered, Ingham joined them from the study. 'You're just in time, John.'

'In time for what?'

'To celebrate.'

'I usually manage to time my entrances well. It's my exits which get the bird.'

Judy's expression was momentarily perplexed because of the way he spoke, but she turned and said to Ingham: 'Why the celebration? Have you just heard something definite from the Nauperts?'

'Contracts are to be drawn up by our respective lawyers and signed as soon as possible. Naupert can't wait to move in. Such a charming house! Such a lovely setting! Exactly what's wanted!'

She fidgeted with her fingers. 'So he couldn't resist … Where do we move to?'

'Ca'na Aloya.' He stared curiously at her. 'You sound as though you'll be sorry to leave here?'

She hesitated. 'Yes, I shall be,' she said finally, and it was clear to Tatham that that was not what she'd been worrying about.

Ingham had not noticed her hesitation. 'I must admit I shall be, as well. This represents the house I'd live in if I could afford to. But beggars can't be choosers, they always tell us. Isn't that right, John?'

'That's the way it goes.'

'Just for once, though, let's prove the old tag wrong. What'll you choose? Any drink you care to name, or a bottle of Moët et Chandon I smuggled in last trip for just such an occasion as this?'

'Nothing but the best for this beggar. The champagne.'

Ingham left the room.

Judy sat down. She stared at the Renoir for a time, then made a conscious effort to forget her own troubled thoughts. 'Have you heard anything more about the funeral, John?'

'Yes. Permission has just been granted.'

'Thank God for that!'

He looked at her, suddenly wondering if she'd suspected anything. 'Why d'you say that?'

She spoke with her usual frankness. 'People were talking more and more. They all love a malicious gossip and when the funeral kept being put off, they had a field day.'

'What were they saying?'

'That Elvina had been informing, telling the Bank of England man about who'd got illegal money out here — as if she'd ever have been an informer. That she'd come into a fortune and so you'd something to do with her death ... Forget 'em. The people haven't anything more intelligent to do. Do you know where to go to make all the arrangements?'

'Yes, thanks. The detective told me.'

'I suppose you realize the English Community will expect to attend in force? To show the flag, they call it.'

'They can go show it somewhere else. This is going to be a very private funeral.'

'I'm glad,' she said simply.

Ingham returned to the room with a bottle of champagne that, having come up from the cellar, was already beginning to frost. He crossed to the bar, opened the door, and went inside.

'John says permission for the funeral has been given,' Judy called out. 'He's keeping it very private.'

Ingham came out with three tulip-shaped glasses and the bottle on a silver tray. 'D'you ever discover, John, why there was all this delay?'

'Not really. All I gathered was, it had to do with the nature of the accident.'

'I'd guess it wasn't anything so definite. If there are two ways of doing a thing out here, they choose the more roundabout one.' He edged the cork out. 'Look at property. They put a tax on a new house which varies according to its value. The owner naturally declares his house is worth only half its real value, the local official levies twice the declared tax, the money paid out and in is right, but everyone feels good because he thinks he's gained one up on the opposition. Can you imagine that attitude prevailing in England?'

'Isn't it a bit like that with us and income tax?'

'Now there's a really dirty word which is never used in polite society out here. In any case, every Englishman is the soul of honour. There isn't one of us who can't put his hand on his heart and swear he's never told a lie to the tax man.'

'But,' said Judy, in a sharp voice, 'could you also swear to having told the whole truth?'

Ingham stared at her briefly and with quick annoyance. But when he spoke, his voice remained light. 'There's a world of subtle difference between the two.' He filled the glasses. He handed her one. 'Stepdaughter, you surprise and sadden me. Haven't you learned that complete morality comes far too expensive for mere mortals? If everyone told all the truth, however, would any business ever be done?' He passed a second glass to Tatham.

'There was a play once, wasn't there, in which everyone did tell the whole truth? What was the ending?'

'I can't remember, but I'm quite sure the entire cast were either murdered or they committed suicide.' Ingham sat down and raised his glass. 'I give you a toast. To the value of silence.'

Looking more sullen than he had ever seen her look before, Judy made no move to drink. But he raised his own glass. For him, too, it was a toast with significant meaning.

CHAPTER XXII

WHEN TATHAM collected the mail from the post office in Llueso on Tuesday, the sixth, there were two letters for him: one from Elvina's solicitors and the other from his mother. The solicitors said that as he was the main beneficiary under his great-aunt's will and as there was every possibility of the inheritance being a fairly considerable one due to the earlier death of her godfather, would he be kind enough to let them know if he would be able to visit their office in the near future in order to begin discussions? His mother wrote that she was sorry to hear Elvina had died in an accident because she'd always found Elvina very amusing and down-to-earth. Also, she'd heard that Knotts Farm, in Letchington, might be coming up for renting next Michaelmas and did he want her to find out more about it: acreage, conditions, terms, etc.?

He strolled back to the square and sat down on one of the wooden seats, not far from the ice-cream stall which had recently started trading.

But for a detective who was at heart a farmer, he'd have written back to ask her to make inquiries as quickly as possible. He thought he could place Knotts Farm. A sober assessment (no rose-tinted spectacles) would go: run down, small fields with overgrown hedges, in a heavily wooded area so that drainage was even more difficult than usual, potential low, virtually guaranteed to kill ambition and strangle success.

What fantastic luck that the investigating detective should have been Enrique Alvarez.

His thoughts returned to the solicitors' letter. He'd write back and say he was returning very soon. Would they be able to assure him that the legal position regarding the inheritance was clear enough for him to start looking for a farm? Inevitably it would take a long time for the money actually to reach him, but equally inevitably it would take him a long time to find the farm he wanted. His mind jumped time. He tramped fields thick with grass, grew crops, bred sleek-hided animals … If only he could start immediately. He'd nothing to hold him on the island. Except … Judy.

The future suddenly seemed far less certain. He'd come to like her a lot. She was warm-natured when she wasn't being bitchy, great fun, and they

156

had found a lot in common. She'd never lived on a farm or had anything to do with farming, yet it was quite reasonable to imagine her in working clothes, sitting on a tractor or helping out in the milking parlour: her smartness was not an end in itself. She preferred to be busy to idleness, admitted to being terrified of poverty and too fond of luxury, but what she really sought was security. But if he proposed to her, would such a proposal denigrate Jennifer's memory? Basically, it was the same question he had asked himself when he had first gone out with Judy on a picnic. He was sure the answer was no, and yet …

He drove back to Ca'n Manin, to find Mayans's battered Citroen 2CV parked alongside the garage and Mayans and his brother-in-law waiting for his return, with the patience of timelessness.

'My brother-in-law,' said the brother-in-law, with a flash of his golden teeth, 'would be happy to know what you will be doing.'

'And so would I.'

The brother-in-law looked bewildered by the answer and so did Mayans when it was translated for him.

'Sit down and I'll get some drinks,' said Tatham. He unlocked the front door and went through to the larder for a bottle of Soberano and three glasses which he put on a tray.

Back on the patio, he poured out three brandies and handed round the glasses. Mayans picked up his glass and drank.

The brother-in-law beamed at Tatham through his spectacles. 'Do you wish for a new lease? It can be a lease for eleven months, but not for a whole year. As it is now the season, if you wish just one month and not eleven, it will be twenty thousand. If you wish two months it will be thirty thousand the second month because then everybodys are after houses.'

Tatham, irritated by such profiteering, suddenly made up his mind. 'I'll be returning home before the tenth, so there's no question of a lease.'

The brother-in-law translated and Mayans broke into a flood of passionate Mallorquin. The brother-in-law removed his spectacles and carefully polished the lenses. He flashed his teeth. 'My brother-in-law says that because he liked the señora so much, he will lease you the house for sixteen thousand for one month, or twenty thousand for the second month.'

'No, thanks.'

The rent drifted downwards. Mayans became more and more excited and finally, with waving hands, he addressed Tatham directly.

'My brother-in-law,' the brother-in-law translated, 'says you are a very fierce businessman and like the señora. May she be peaceful. He says he loved the señora. So he will charge you twelve thousand a month for eleven months, but please tell other peoples fifteen thousand, or twenty if they are important peoples.'

'But I keep telling you, I'm not staying here. I'm going home.'

Mayans stood up. He stared at Tatham, scratched his curly black hair, and suddenly beamed. He spoke rapidly, but briefly.

'My brother-in-law thinks perhaps you like buy this house. For you, but for no other peoples, it will cost five million.'

Tatham smiled. 'Thanks, but I'm going home to buy a farm — I still have to work for a living.'

'A big farm, you will be buying?'

'No, it'll only be a small one. Maybe seventy to a hundred hectares.'

He'd forgotten that on this island a farm of five hectares was large. They left, obviously convinced he was a liar and respecting him for doing everything possible to beat down the proposed rent.

He carried the brandy and three glasses into the kitchen. He lit a cigarette. He'd told them he was returning home at once and so be it. The future as it lay between himself and Judy must be left to the future.

One of the things he must do before leaving was to sort out the furniture and effects and have anything of value-stored until it was certain what was to be done with it. He went upstairs and into Elvina's bedroom.

There were a few pieces of jewellery in a battered leather case: he was no judge of jewellery, so it must be expertly examined. In one drawer of the chest-of-drawers was a pile of letters, perhaps twenty in all, written many years before, with envelopes browned with age: he put them on the floor for burning. Most of the clothes were also only fit for burning, but there was one fur coat that looked of fairly good quality and was hung in a large plastic bag: unless it were mink, which even to his eyes seemed unlikely, it could be offered to Catalina who would appreciate the memento even if this was not a country where a fur coat was often worn. In a drawer were several children's books, all dated in pen on the fly leaves, which had been hers when young. With pages torn and drawn on in coloured pencils, these could be of no value to anyone else. He put them on the burning pile.

In the solar, he first went over to the desk. It contained surprisingly little. Three folders of receipts and official documents, some recent letters from friends in England awaiting answering, a pocket Spanish/English dictionary, and several ancient guarantee cards which dated from when she'd first come. Apart from the desk, there were two empty suitcases stored above the staircase and, of course, the carpets. He could remember clearly her saying to him: 'Those two are Ispahan, quite old, and I suppose rather valuable. That one is a Gum and Paul gave it to me on our first wedding anniversary. That other is supposed to be a Mir, but a friend of Paul's came and was certain it was an Abadah. I never bothered to sort out their identifications. I just like them all, although I really like the Gum most of all for sentimental reasons.' Unless she had willed them to someone else, he would lay them in the farmhouse. They would be something personal of hers.

Then, as he stared at them, he abruptly realized that she would never have walked over them in muddy shoes.

CHAPTER XXIII

ALVAREZ EXAMINED his nails and noticed without surprise that they were unusually dirty. Then he looked across his desk at Tatham and his expression was one of irritation. 'You tell me she would never have walked over those carpets on the Friday?'

'She'd not have walked over any carpets in such muddy shoes,' replied Tatham, 'because she had a thing about keeping the house clean and tidy. But those carpets held tremendous sentimental value for her, over and above their high intrinsic value, so she would never have dreamed of going on them with shoes caked with sticky mud.'

'Yet carpets are for walking on.'

'Not these: not for her.'

Alvarez didn't understand, and yet he did. He remembered he'd been attracted by the beauty of the four carpets when he'd briefly seen them.

Tatham spoke more urgently. 'You can't get out on to the balcony without walking on them. If it was fine and one's shoes were clean, that was all right — a little walking on them may have done them some good. But Elvina was wearing thick walking shoes, caked with mud from the dirt-track, and on top of that going out on to the wet balcony would have made them worse. She'd never have returned from a walk, gone upstairs, crossed the carpets, and gone out on to the balcony in those shoes.'

Alvarez spoke with the tired fatalism of someone trying to avoid the unavoidable. 'Could she not have worn the shoes when clean and have walked out on to the balcony and made them dirty there?'

Tatham shook his head. 'I've just told you — and you must have seen for yourself, unless the sea washed it all off — the dirt on the shoes came from the track round to the road.'

Alvarez sighed. 'So?'

Tatham hesitated, then spoke very quickly. 'There's been something wrong from the beginning. You told me her last meal was very light, mainly bread, and she'd had no alcohol for at least nine hours. But it's impossible to think of her having lunch without a drink or two and plenty of wine ... She cannot have eaten lunch.'

160

'Are you suggesting, then, she died before lunch, in the middle of the day? That is impossible. Catalina, the maid, was at the house between three and five and there was certainly no body on the patio then.'

Tatham, voice slightly hoarse, asked: 'How soon does rigor mortis start?'

Alvarez shrugged his shoulders.

'Can you find out?'

Alvarez, looking more tired than ever, his clothes sagging round him, stood up and crossed to the small bookcase from which he brought the text-book on forensic medicine. He returned to his chair, checked the index, turned the pages, and read a couple of paragraphs. He looked up. 'Describe as exactly as you can remember the state of your aunt's body when you lifted it.'

'I'd parked the car so the lights were on her. Her head was pointing towards the car. Her arms were outstretched and when I first tried to tuck them in to her sides they refused to move. Her legs were stiff also, though not so stiff as her arms, and it was a job to fold up her body.'

'Then rigor had spread down her body to her legs and that normally takes between seven to nine hours.'

'Which puts her death at between one and three in the afternoon.'

'Or conditions were abnormal.' Alvarez jabbed his finger down on the book. 'It says that rigor is a very unreliable guide to the time of death.'

'Then don't forget something else. The meal was eaten two hours before her death. She had a very late breakfast. That fits in with the rigor times. She ate bread and butter only, and drank coffee. That fits.'

Alvarez scratched his right ear. 'Didn't you say there was a great deal of blood on the patio?'

'I said there was relatively little. But there should have been a great deal, shouldn't there? That alone could have suggested the truth.'

'What is the truth?'

'She died somewhere else and was brought to the house after Catalina had left and was pushed through the wooden rails of the balcony to make it seem she had met her death there, at home.'

'If that were true, the person who brought her body back would have expected its discovery soon to become news. When it didn't, he or she would have become desperate to know why. Did anyone come the next day, asking for the señora, trying to find out where she was?'

Tatham thought back. 'No. No one came here.'

Alvarez shut the book with a snap. 'My father was a very realistic man. One day, when I was young, I asked him why there were stars in the sky? He told me, "Why bother about the answer? It can do us no good. Instead, bother about why all the melons are this year splitting. The answer to that will do us good."'

Tatham fidgeted with a coin in the right-hand pocket of the light-weight trousers he was wearing. 'But you are saying ...'

'I am saying that you went to a great deal of trouble to conceal the time of the señora's death. Yet you come with questions which can only be answered by destroying all you have worked for. Convince me the señora was killed in some manner other than an accidental fall from the balcony and I must investigate because it may be a case of murder. Immediately, everyone must know the señora died not on the twenty-fifth of April, but on the sixteenth. Did you not tell me that then the farm of your dreams can never be?'

'Yes, but ...'

'But what, Señor?'

'If she was murdered — as she must have been ...'

'Must have been? Let us suppose she died somewhere else, in a different manner. Could it not have been an accident which someone had to conceal, just as you thought there had been an accident which you had to conceal?'

'But you've got to make certain whether it was an accident or whether it was murder.'

'Why?'

'If there's been a murder, the murderer's got to be caught.'

'Again I ask you, why?'

'But ...' Tatham stared at him, shocked by the question.

'Is it revenge you seek? But that will not restore your aunt to life. So the only result will be to destroy your own future life.'

'It's not revenge. It's that justice be done.'

'What is the real difference? And who are you to call for justice, when you tried so hard to defeat it? And did you not tell me all that justice did not do for you in England?'

'If it was a murder and the murderer gets away with it ...'

'He will spend the rest of his life worried that the truth will one day arrive and he will be caught. Punishment enough.'

'But in God's name, what would happen if every crime committed were ignored like that?'

'You are forgetting, this is not an ordinary crime — if it is a real crime. If the señora was murdered, the murderer is a man or woman of high intelligence and cunning or he or she would not have thought of faking an accident. Or think of placing the bamboo to explain away the particular injury to her head, should anyone ever doubt the accident and demand a post-mortem. A person of intelligence murders only when it is absolutely necessary. Therefore this is an isolated case and will lead to no other crimes. The course of justice for others will not be altered if the murderer goes unidentified.

'Señor,' continued Alvarez earnestly, 'remember the melons my father spoke about. Go back to England and buy that farm. Give the señora the memorial she longed for.'

Tatham slowly stood up. Only on this island could a detective argue someone out of presenting evidence which tended to prove that a murder had been committed.

*

Tatham poured himself out another gin and tonic, conscious even as he did so that he had already drunk enough to blur his thinking. He returned to the sitting-room and slumped down in one of the chairs. What did he do? On the one hand a fortune, but bury the truth: on the other, discover the truth, but bury the fortune. Should he, as Alvarez said, forget the stars and concentrate on the melons?

He drank. Might not Elvina for once have gone upstairs in filthy shoes? Surely no one ever acted consistently all the time? Might she not earlier have suddenly felt ill so that she had no lunch? Might she not have bled profusely, but he remembered incorrectly? Might the rigor mortis, notoriously unreliable, not have taken an unusual course?

He looked at his glass and was surprised to discover it was empty. He went through to the pantry and refilled it.

Murder postulated a motive. Who had a motive to murder Elvina? Mayans, clearly. At her death, the lease of the house had expired and now he was able to ask a very much higher rent. The Mallorquins were crazy for money. The Eastmores? On the face of it, an unlikely possibility yet Catalina — source of so much information on the other English — had told Elvina that they were very worried because some bank official had come from England and was making financial inquiries. Local gossip had named Elvina the informer. If the Eastmores had been worried, it suggested they'd something to hide and perhaps they'd believed Elvina was an informer and had killed her to prevent her informing on them. They were the leaders of the English Community. As such, they must be seen to be beyond reproach.

Alvarez had made the point that if Elvina had been murdered, or had suffered an accident elsewhere, the murderer, or the witness to her accident, must have been desperate to know what had happened to her body. Both Mayans and Lady Eastmore had come to the house to speak to Elvina, but not until the Friday, nine days after she'd actually died. (Of course, one or other of them might have called when he was out on his 'picnics with Elvina'.) Alvarez had also said that this third person would have to be of high intelligence and cunning. Mayans was cunning but not highly intelligent; the Eastmores were highly intelligent but not cunning.

He couldn't explain even to himself what it was he wanted — revenge, justice, an easy conscience? — yet even if it was right against his own interests, he had to try to find out the truth. And, his gin-scrambled brain said, he had to know now. He left the house and climbed into the Fiat. He must drive very carefully. He was quite certain he was in sufficient control of himself to drive, even if the Spanish police were murder on drunken drivers. The thing was, he wasn't anywhere near tight …

He decided he must have been very deep in thought because he found himself entering the drive of Ca'n Lluxa without any clear recollection of the short journey. That worried him for a little, but he very soon forgot it. He climbed out.

He rang the front-door bell, hammered on the brass knocker, rang the bell again in case no one had heard him the first twice. Miguel, looking flustered, opened the door and spoke a flood of Spanish.

'Sure, I'll come in,' said Tatham. He stepped inside. He tripped over something and almost fell.

Miguel spoke again, gesturing with his hands. 'Sure, I'll come along,' said Tatham. 'I want a word with them, but I rather doubt they'll want a word with me. Where are they?'

Miguel began to speak again, then shrugged his shoulders. They heard a laugh which came from their right. Only Lady Eastmore could laugh like that, Tatham decided. He crossed the hall, opened a door, stepped inside, and tripped. He saved himself by grabbing the comer of the unusually large Hepplewhite table. There was a clink of silver (George IV, Queen's pattern, engraved with the Eastmores' crest of a boar's head) as the table shook.

Four people sat round the table: the Eastmores and Brigadier and Mrs Cabbott. They were wearing light-weight suits and formal dresses and the women had on some of their better jewellery. They looked like, he decided, an advertisement for one of the old-fashioned savoury spreads.

Miguel stood in the doorway and spoke with nervous haste.

'Good afternoon,' said Lady Eastmore. 'No doubt you did not understand that Miguel was trying to tell you that we were engaged?'

'That's right,' he answered thickly. He had discovered what he most disliked about her. It was her invincible self-control in the face of every and any situation.

'However, now that you have seen for yourself that we are engaged, you will wish to leave.'

'No, I don't. I want to talk to you.'

'For the moment, I regret I cannot return the compliment. If it has somehow escaped your notice, we are in the middle of our luncheon.'

'I'm not worried.'

'Mr Tatham, you force me to be very blunt. Will you kindly leave?'

'Not till I've said what I've come to say.'

Brigadier Cabbott laughed loudly.

'Freddie!' snapped his wife.

Lord Eastmore stood up and spoke with stem authority. 'My wife has been very patient ...'

'I'll bet she hasn't got the passion not to be.'

'This is utterly outrageous,' gasped Mrs Cabbott. 'I have never met such ill manners. Never. Ever.'

'D'you know what the real trouble is?' said Cabbott, with great glee. 'The nig-nog's as pissed as a coot!' He began to laugh, then cried out. 'Christ! You've broken my ankle.'

Mrs Cabbott leaned forward to hiss a warning at him that if he didn't shut up she'd break a lot more and her right breast knocked over her wine glass. Wine spilled out over the highly polished table and there was a cry of anguish from Lady Eastmore, who hurriedly stood up to mop up the wine with her table napkin. She cannoned into Miguel who was rushing to help. Tatham began to laugh and couldn't stop for some time.

He discovered that Lord Eastmore now stood by his side. 'You'd better leave,' said Lord Eastmore harshly.

'And you'd better listen to me.' Tatham tried to cast from his memory the elan with which Mrs Cabbott's imprisoned right breast had knocked over the wine glass, but he giggled once more before he said: 'I know you know a great deal about Elvina's death. Much more than you've ever let on.'

Lady Eastmore handed Miguel the stained napkin and returned to her chair. 'Charles, the man must be mentally deranged.'

'Nonsense,' said Cabbott. 'I told you. He's just plain bloody pi — tight.'

'How could he come *here*?' cried Mrs Cabbott. 'To this house of all houses. It's ... it's lèse-majesté.'

'You know when she really died, don't you?' demanded Tatham.

They stared at him.

'And you know how she really died. That's why you kept calling at Ca'n Manin to discover what had happened to her body when her death wasn't announced.'

'We'd a bloke like this once.' said Cabbott. 'Out in Iraq ... Or was it Syria? ... Or maybe it was Suez?'

'For heaven's sake, it doesn't matter where it was,' snapped Mrs Cabbott.

'Yes, it does, old dear. Very hot. Everybody thirsty. Bloke snuffed it after boozing home-brewed ploop. Spent three days in sick-bay, screaming a load of balls like this nig-nog. Nice bloke, too.'

Tatham let go of the table and almost fell. He grabbed it again. 'How did she really die? Where?'

'I think, Charles, we have no option but to call the police,' said Lady Eastmore. 'And no doubt they will be interested in what he's saying.'

'I'm afraid you're right, dear,' said Lord Eastmore.

'You're bluffing,' said Tatham. 'You daren't call them along.'

There was a telephone on the corner of the very elegant sideboard. Lord Eastmore walked over to it.

They weren't bluffing, decided Tatham. Any minute now, Lord Eastmore would call the police. Which meant that they weren't scared of a further investigation which, in turn, must mean they had had nothing to do with, and knew nothing about Elvina's death.

'I think,' said Lady Eastmore, 'that Mr Tatham has decided to leave without any further unseemly behaviour.'

He stared at her. 'That's right, I'm leaving.'

'Kindly do so immediately. And please do not call here again,' she said, with polite distaste. 'The staff will ...'

'Stuff the staff.'

'Keep off the cheap gin,' called out Cabbott with undiminished cheerfulness. 'Out here, they make it from petrol.'

He walked into the hall and Miguel accompanied him, Miguel raised his right hand.

'All right, all right, I'm going nice and quietly, and there's no need to throw me out.'

Miguel shook his hand with enthusiasm, opened the door, and bowed with great courtesy as he left.

Strangely, the fresh air seemed to sober him sufficiently that by the time he reached the Fiat he was more in control of his limbs. He sat down behind the wheel and started the engine.

The drive took him past Ca'n Xema and when he saw the drystone house, looking very beautiful in the sunlight, he suddenly decided to see Judy. He turned off the road and then saw, for the first time, that there was a car parked in the drive. As he came to a halt, Ingham and another man stepped out of the house.

The second man looked slightly familiar. But why? Small, dumpy with a paunch, a Vandyke beard … Ingham shook hands with the man, who climbed into a bright orange Seat 600 and then lowered the window and talked, his beard moving rapidly. The waggling beard triggered off Tatham's memory. Ca'n Manin, the night of Good Friday. He'd been waiting for Judy because they'd been going into Llueso for the procession and there'd been a knock on the front door. He'd gone into the hall expecting the caller to be Judy, but it had been this man with the waggling Vandyke beard. Elvina had said that something about the man reminded her of his father, but had never detailed what. But now he knew. The man was a painter.

CHAPTER XXIV

INGHAM BROUGHT the coffee into the sitting-room, where Tatham sat on the settee. 'Strong and black and from the look of you, you need it.'

Tatham drank half the coffee. He lit a cigarette. 'That man who left when I arrived is a painter, isn't he?'

Ingham went across to the bar and poured himself out a brandy. When he returned, he settled in one of the armchairs.

'Isn't he?' repeated Tatham.

Ingham looked at Tatham with sharp speculation, then answered the question. 'According to himself, he's a genius. As yet unrecognized by a Philistine world.'

'And he painted the Renoir for you?'

The lines around Ingham's mouth tightened and he looked cruel rather than dissipated. 'Presumably Judy has been confiding in you?'

'Only because she was so desperately worried on your account.'

'She need not have been.'

'She was scared you were trying to sell a fake Renoir to Naupert as genuine. I proved to her it couldn't be the case.' Ingham clipped the end of a cigar with great care. He lit it. 'Do I owe you my thanks for testifying to my honesty?' Tatham ignored the mocking question. 'I said you were selling a fake as a fake, to a buyer who was secretly certain lie was buying the genuine article. I doubted that was a criminal offence.'

Ingham lifted his glass of brandy and drank.

'Isn't that the way it went?'

'Does it really matter?'

'It matters a great deal. After all, that man, carrying a parcel the size and shape of the Renoir, called at Ca'n Manin on Good Friday, thinking he was here. Elvina instinctively identified him as a painter.'

'She was always an acute woman.'

'Acute enough to wonder why a wealthy, hard-headed German industrialist should think of buying a house for more than it was worth on the open market. Acute enough to remember the painter who had under his arm a parcel that looked like a painting. Acute enough to remember what paintings were hanging on the walls of this room when she and I came along for drinks.'

'Is all this of any relevancy?'

'It's highly relevant when one knows that Elvina died on Wednesday, the sixteenth.'

'You must have drunk a lot more than ...'

'I'm sober enough to know exactly what I'm saying. On the sixteenth, Judy and I went out on a picnic. When I returned to Ca'n Manin in the evening, I found Elvina had apparently fallen from the balcony on to the patio and was dead. Because of an inheritance she'd promised to give to me, due from her godfather, who although on the point of death had not yet died, I had to conceal her death.

'Eventually, the cable announcing his death came and I arranged for her "death" on that night. I wasn't nearly as clever as I thought I'd been and the police became suspicious, but in the end I was able to persuade them that her death had been in order. It all seemed over and done with. Then I suddenly realized Elvina would never have crossed the carpets in the solar in her filthy outdoor shoes. After discovering one inconsistency, I discovered others ... Added together, they had to mean she'd died elsewhere and had been carried to the patio to fake an accident there.

'It's taken me until now to appreciate certain facts about the faking — but then I'm really only at home with the problems of cows. First off, was the timing. The person who took her body to Ca'n Manin must have known that Catalina worked there from three until five. He also knew I was out and wouldn't return until fairly late in the evening. Most of the English probably knew the first fact, only you and Judy knew for certain the second.

'The person who faked the accident had to be clever and cunning, so much so that he even introduced a length of bamboo on which she supposedly fell — there was a chance in a hundred a post-mortem would be held, a chance in a thousand the blow to the skull which had been made with a blunt instrument the size of the bamboo would have left a mark that despite the extensive injuries would be discovered and identified.

'There had to be a motive and a strong one. Two lots of people seemed to have motives. I saw the Eastmores earlier on and was on my way to the Mayans when I stopped here and met for the second time the painter. Having identified him, I knew a third person had a motive — you. Elvina loved prying into other people's affairs and it intrigued her to learn how you'd interested Naupert into offering twenty million for this house. But she was also an honest person — it was the essential dishonesty of the social pattern that she found so contemptible — and once she divined what your plan was, she was determined to stop it. But because she was so straightforward, she came to tell you face to face what she intended so that if you had enough sense you could pack in your plans. Twenty million pesetas were your motive.

'Having set up a fake accident, you were on tenterhooks until you could be certain everything had gone according to plan. But there was no report of any accident and Elvina was supposedly still alive. Only one person, for reasons that couldn't have been clear, could have been concealing her death and that person was me. So you were desperate to know what had happened, but far too cunning to quiz me directly in case I ever became in the slightest degree suspicious. You encouraged Judy to see me so that you could pump her to find out what was happening.'

Ingham smoked for a while, then he said: 'Is the inheritance a large one?'

'I believe so.'

'And it's now yours?'

'Provided no one challenges the two wills.'

'Then you daren't do anything to upset the date of Elvina's death.' It was a flat statement.

'The fact that I'm here must show that I dare.'

'It shows only that you dare to try to discover the truth, not that you'll publish that truth. You're not going to throw a fortune away.'

'Aren't I?'

'What is it? Do you think I murdered her?'

'Probably.'

'You think me capable of murdering a defenceless old woman, just to protect the sale of this house for twenty million …? I suppose there are times when murder would come easily: marriage certainly provides innumerable possible occasions. But I liked Elvina far too much ever to have harmed her. I may be unprincipled in some respects, but I still honour my friends.'

'Then what happened?'

'You've guessed most of what happened. Or would you prefer me to say, deduced …? Elvina came here and told me in her inimitable style that she wasn't going to let me make a fool out of Naupert. I was surprised. What is a rich German industrialist good for, if not for making a fool out of? But

I'd underrated Elvina. Beneath that Bohemian exterior, there lurked a Calvinistic soul — in so far as honesty was concerned. I told her she was being rather stupid because if a clever German liked to lose five million by trying to swindle me that was his funeral and she should just enjoy the laugh. But she got really ratty, as if I'd impugned her chastity, and ...' He stopped.

'And what?'

He stood up, placed the glass on the small table by the side of his chair, crossed to the large fireplace, turned, puffed at the cigar, and then said: 'I was here, when I told her she was being stupid. She became wildly excited, grabbed my arm and said that, stupid or not, she was going to blow the gaff if I tried to go ahead.

'Selling this place for twenty million represented the difference between losing everything — the law out here doesn't exactly favour a foreigner — and continuing my pleasant life and making a sizeable fortune on my other properties. To tell the truth, I got annoyed at her threats and unrealistic attitude and when she grabbed me, I jerked my arm free with too much force.'

He was silent for a few seconds. 'I hate what happened. I keep remembering every second ...' He looked up at Tatham. 'I'd unintentionally used so much force that she spun round, tripped, and fell. She hit her head on one of the fire-dogs and when I checked, she was dead. It was that sudden.'

Tatham stared at the two fire-dogs and the firebasket, almost certainly English in origin. The long arms of the dogs were about two centimetres in diameter.

'I was frightened sick, both by what had happened and by what it seemed must follow.' Ingham returned to his chair, sat down, and picked up his glass. 'I'm certainly not proud of the way I thought, but ... Well, you must have gone through the same kind of mental hell ... If I called in the police, they'd ask questions and what convincing reason for what had happened could I give except the truth? That would be the end of the twenty million for this house. Even if I somehow managed to lie successfully to the police, I'd no idea how much Elvina had discussed with you. So I reckoned my only way out was to repeat what had actually happened, an accident, but make it seem to have happened at your house. Then there'd be no suspicion I was involved.

'So now we both know, for the first time, all of the truth. And there's obviously no need for anyone else ever to know it. There was a terrible accident, but nothing we do can turn back the clock. If we forget all we know, I'll sell this house for more than it's worth to a man who can easily afford to lose a few millions and is trying to swindle me, you gain your inheritance which was meant to come through to you but won't if the truth ever leaks out. You know something? Elvina was far too sharp a realist ever to want any other conclusion to all that's happened.'

Tatham felt guilty because he was so desperately relieved. The farm was finally and forever his ... An accident was different from a murder. Ingham was right: Elvina would never have wanted the truth to come out about the tragic accident.

Whilst they were still both silent, they heard the front door open. Judy's voice called out: 'Hi! Where are you?'

'We're here,' replied Ingham.

She came in. 'Hallo, John. I was glad to find the car outside because I was going to call you. I've been given two tickets to a concert in Palma tonight — Brahms, Chopin, and Beethoven. I'm hoping you'll use the second one?'

He stared at her without answering.

'What on earth's the matter?' she asked.

Ingham chuckled. 'Nothing, Judy, that a brisk walk up the valley won't cure. He's just had a heavy session and is recovering from my blackest of black coffee.'

'John! Surely you're not going to join the soaks brigade? The best thing for you is what Larry's just suggested-a really good, sharp walk. So on to your feet, sir, and no rest for the first twenty kilometres.'

Obediently he stood up.

'I must say, you look quite awful! Where have you been boozing?'

'Mostly on my own,' he replied, 'but I ended up at the Eastmores'.'

'You're a glutton for punishment.'

'I can't remember very clearly, but I think I made a bit of a scene and was rather rude.'

'To her very noble ladyship?' She laughed. 'Then you'll be ostracized and recommended for deportation. I didn't know you had it in you, but I'm delighted to discover you have. Come on, we'll be off before you're too rude to me. What shoes have you on ...? They'll be good enough because it's not rough walking, but I'd better change into something a little stouter.'

She left the room. Tatham followed her after a last look at Ingham, whose face held a sardonic smile. To the right of the hall was a built-in cupboard and from this she brought out a pair of brogues. 'Can you give me some support while I change my shoes, or is standing still an impossible feat right now?

He gave her support and she changed her shoes. She then stepped into the cupboard and searched for something. After a time, she put her head outside and called: 'Larry.'

'Yes,' he shouted back.

'Where's your walking-stick?'

There was quite a long pause. 'I lost it some time ago.'

'You never told me that.' She stepped out of the cupboard, shut the door and led the way out of the house. As they began to walk down the drive, she linked her arm with his and said: 'He's had that stick for years and years. Reckons it brings him luck because he bought it from an old gipsy who spat and blessed it. Funny his not being more upset about losing it.'

'What ... what size was it?' he asked.

'Why? Have you seen one lying around somewhere?'

He shook his head. 'How thick was it?' he persisted.

'About like that.' She joined forefinger and thumb to show a circle about two centimetres in diameter. 'We'll have to try and get him another. Provided one of us spits on it, that should be all right ... John, what on earth's now going on in that head of yours?'

'A hell of a headache.'

'You're not getting out of a walk that easily! Come on, step it out. As my old virgin schoolmistress used to tell us all, there's nothing like a good walk to make you less liable to think nasty thoughts.'

He walked with her in the hot sunshine, but his thoughts remained nasty.

CHAPTER XXV

SPREIGHT FARM lay on rich, well-drained loam. The fields were large following the dragging up of many thorn hedges, but care had been taken to leave sufficient hedging to retain character and prevent any wind erosion. The new variety of rye grass was growing very strongly and it promised two tons of hay, or the equivalent, to the acre. There was enough spare land beyond the cows' grass requirements to grow barley and oats, both of which did well on the soil, and enough drying and storage space for all that might be harvested. The equipment was extremely good. Automatic bulk feeding of silage, automatic slurry disposal out to the fields, bulk milk tank, herringbone parlour, cow kennels, mill and pelleter, Dutch barns, hay elevators, 165 and 135 MF tractors, high-output bailer, forage harvester, flail mower, hay conditioner … One hundred and seventy-five glossy-flanked Friesians, milk average steadily climbing, twenty-five followers to premium bulls … Pilot bull beef scheme showing a first-class foot input to weight increase ratio …

It was the farm of Tatham's dreams. He and Basil — chosen after interviewing nearly twenty applicants and almost as dedicated as himself — ran it, only having to call in contract labour at the peak work times of the year.

In April, when the morning air was sharp and sparkling and the sunshine was chased across the countryside by merry puffballs of cumulus, Tatham — having risen at five to milk — ate his usual large breakfast: two eggs, three rashers of bacon, three tomatoes, two pieces of fried bread, toast, and marmalade, three cups of coffee. He read the morning newspaper which was propped up against the coffee jug.

Mrs Willow, small, thin, slightly cross-eyed, far jollier than her features suggested, looked into the dining-room. 'Anything more wanted?'

'No, thanks, Mrs Willow.'

'I'll be off to the village to do the shopping, then.' She left.

She reminded him of a chirpy sparrow, hopping here and there and always busy. She came all day, six days a week, grateful now that her husband was dead to earn a good wage.

174

He finished the last piece of toast, poured out the final cup of coffee, and lit a cigarette. For the moment he stopped reading and leaned back in his chair, stretched out his legs, and looked round the room. Oak-beamed ceiling, one wall oak-beamed, inglenook fireplace with seats and places for warming the pewter mugs of ale ... Elvina would have loved the mellow beauty of this farmhouse, just as she would have loved the farm. She would have chosen no different memorial. And inside five years, he'd prove his boast to her.

Satisfied with his world, he resumed reading the paper and almost immediately he saw a short paragraph which made him start with surprise. He read it through a second timje and then he pushed back the chair, stood up, and walked over to the east window. He stared out at the untidy garden — no true farmer ever had time to mess around with a garden.

His troubled thoughts were interrupted by a knock on the front door. Basil stepped into the hall. 'John, are you there?'

He crossed the room to the hall, once the outshot and whose roof reached up to the galleried landing above. Basil, dressed in open-necked shirt and jeans, said: 'D'you want me to start the cows off in the new paddock?'

'Yeah,' he answered vaguely.

A puzzled look crossed Basil's face. 'Anything the matter?'

'Not really, just a bit of unexpected news.' Tatham spoke more briskly. 'Can you manage the cows on your own? There's something I want to do.'

'Sure, just so long as that old wall-eyed cow which is bulling doesn't start getting too frisky.' He left.

Tatham stayed in the hall. He lit a cigarette. That paragraph in the paper had somehow, in a subtle manner he couldn't begin to define, made up his mind for him after weeks and months of indecision. He entered the sitting-room — more oak beams, roughly shaped this time — and crossed the Mir — or was it an Abadah? — carpet to the telephone. He dialled the international exchange and gave the number, Llueso 383. Miraculously, there was no delay. Scraps of Spanish, a couple of sharp clicks, and then the ringing began.

'Hullo,' said Judy. 'Llueso three eight three.'

'Judy, it's John. John Tatham.'

There was a pause. 'I thought you'd forgotten how to get in touch with me. I sent you via your mother the card with our new address and telephone number and never heard a word.'

'I'd apologize, only I don't feel all that sorry: I needed time to think.'

'I see. And having thought?'

'I wondered if you'd like to fly over and see the farm?'

The words came in a rush. 'Yes, I would. Is tomorrow too soon? If I can get a flight. What's it like and are you happy? Are the cows giving all the milk they should?'

'They're doing so well you can have a bath in milk if that's what you'd like. Ring me when you get a booking and I'll meet the plane — always provided it doesn't clash with milking time, of course.'

'Of course!' She laughed. 'I know my place in English farming society.'

'That's good. Can I have a word now with Lawrence?'

'You may, provided that when you've finished talking to him I can have another word with you.'

'It's a deal.'

After a short pause, Ingham said: 'Hullo, John.'

'Lawrence, I've just read something in the *Daily Telegraph* I thought you'd be interested to hear. Herr Naupert has sold a Renoir he discovered in Mallorca, authenticated by two leading art experts in Germany, to the Backenhoff Gallery in Essen for just under one million marks. You can tell your friend with the Vandyke beard that he really is the genius he calls himself.'

There was no comment.

Judy came back on the phone. 'John, what on earth have you said to Larry to send him stamping off, looking as though he'd had his liver cut out?'

'Only that a mutual friend has come into rather a lot of money.'

'Obviously, it's someone he doesn't like … John, where is the farm? D'you realize I haven't even got its address? I've sat and stared at a map of England and wondered whether you were sitting on a stool with straws in your hair and milking cows into a dirty old bucket in Devon or Yorkshire or Norfolk …'

Printed in Great Britain
by Amazon

81616197R00103